SPECTRE

*For Sarah
From Prussia with Love*
[signature]
Feb 18, 2015

SPECTRE
LAURENCE A. RICKELS

FORT WAYNE, INDIANA

SPECTRE
Copyright © 2013 by Laurence A. Rickels
ISBN: 978-0-9892391-1-0
Library of Congress Control Number: 2013954123

First Anti-Oedipal Paperback Edition, November 2013

All rights reserved. No part of this book may be reproduced, stored in a retrieval system, or transmitted by any means without the written permission of the author and publisher. Published in the United States by Anti-Oedipus Press, an imprint of Hawgstrüffel Media Group, Inc.

Cover Design © 2013 by Matthew Revert
www.MatthewRevert.com

Layout by D. Harlan Wilson
www.DHarlanWilson.com

Anti-Oedipus Press
Fort Wayne, IN

www.Anti-OedipusPress.com

OTHER BOOKS BY LAURENCE A. RICKELS

I Think I Am: Philip K. Dick
The Devil Notebooks
Ulrike Ottinger: The Autobiography of Art Cinema
Nazi Psychoanalysis, Vol. 1: Only Psychoanalysis Won the War
Nazi Psychoanalysis, Vol. 2: Crypto-Fetishism
Nazi Psychoanalysis, Vol. 3: Psy-Fi
The Vampire Lectures
The Case of California
Aberrations of Mourning: Writing on German Crypts

PRAISE FOR THE WORK OF LAURENCE A. RICKELS

Aberrations of Mourning

"For Rickels, the link between technology and mourning isn't merely Freudian and speculative, but also solidly historically grounded. In his excellent book *Aberrations of Mourning*, he points to the advent in the west of recording devices such as phonographs and gramophones before in fact mortality rates had been reduced by mass inoculation, even among the better off. Many middle-class parents, following the fad for recording their children's voices, found themselves bereaved, and the plate or roll on which little Augustus' or Matilda's voice outlived him or her thus became a tomb. 'Dead children,' Rickels writes, 'inhabit vaults of the technical media which create them.' Bereavement becomes the core of technologies; what communication technology inaugurates is, in effect, a cult of mourning—indeed, Rickels even suggests replacing the word 'mourning' with the phrase 'the audio and video broadcasts of improper burial'... Researching my own novel *C*, which takes place during precisely this period of emergence, I found evidence everywhere to support Rickels' claim."

— **Tom McCarthy**

Nazi Psychoanalysis

"He brilliantly traces discourses on the relationship between pilots and their aircraft, spinning out all kinds of associations around men and machines, treating psychoanalysis as a kind of privileged discourse on the 'ongoing technologization of our bodies' that ran through the twentieth century."

— **Paul Lerner, University of Southern California**

"The author's knowledge of his own writing seems to produce a form of textuality that is forever sliding into the category of materiality... The author of *Nazi Psychoanalysis* has sought to develop a style that holds the line between a concern for content and a preoccupation with form in order to fight the restrictive nature of the modern symbolic order... Rickels' liminal textuality combines the normal position of the analyst and the dislocated situation of the patient in a mode of writing that is always-already becoming coherent/incoherent. This is the mark of what I want to call his post-modern schizo-style... Rickels' schizo-style allows us to see how psycho-pathologies emerge from the same hyper-reflexive modern moment that gave birth to psychoanalysis itself."

— **Mark Featherstone, Keele University**

I Think I Am: Philip K. Dick

"A Deleuzoguattarian rhizome that deterritorializes a wide array of psychic, anthropological and literary assemblages, *I Think I Am: Philip K. Dick* is the most compelling and philosophically creative book in the growing library of PKD Studies."

— *Extrapolation*

"Rickels does not force the fictions into the mold of his mostly psychoanalytic concepts, but rather bounces the concepts off the texts and leaves the reader to work out what they have dislodged."

— *Science Fiction Studies*

"Rickels does not merely invite readers to see Dick's work the way he does; instead, the theoretical framework invites a broader vision that includes and projects outward from science fiction and fantasy."

— *Studies in Popular Culture*

"Aside from its perfect fit of critic and subject, Laurence A. Rickels' book provides the most thorough and exhaustive reading of Philip K. Dick's literary work that exists. He goes through all the novels literally, both the science fiction works and the so-called mainstream novels Dick did not publish in his lifetime. The reader of science fiction should welcome a book like this, which is both knowledgeable of the SF tradition and creatively analytical. I could not put this book down once I began to read it."

— **George Slusser, University of California-Riverside**

ACKNOWLEDGEMENTS

Just when I thought I had been cast out of U.S. academic publishing like an older, no-longer-cute pet, I was discovered and rescued by a writer, D. Harlan Wilson, to appear alongside other bona fide writers in his new press. Burn bridges burn! *SPECTRE* nonetheless has a history. The invitation to deliver the 2007 Otto and Ilse Mainzer Lecture at New York University provided the occasion to sift through my teaching-related encounters with James Bond and the Superhuman and to bring into the foreground the underlying reading of Melanie Klein and her crypt. The James Bond paper, more or less, appeared in German translation as the central panel of my 2012 book *Geprüfte Seelen*, a title that is a Daniel Paul Schreber citation: "tested souls." It was flanked by more exploration of the concept of reality testing, but within the corpus of Philip K. Dick.

The chain of signifiers I pulled as Mainzer Lecturer I thought entitled my Bond reading, since already imbued with acceptance, to catch up with one of those standing invitations I guess I alone take seriously. But it turned out that the initials of the name drop stood for "culture industry." How could the "die messages" (as P. K. Dick would say) pummeling me in my work environment at UC-Santa Barbara, from the department throughout the hierarchy of the administration, driving me to get lost, not be networked with all the other coordinates of the academic world? It's a small-minded world after all. "Sentence by sentence we enjoyed many of your insights, but there was also some wondering at just whether there would be any limit to the puns you are willing to pull out of the hat." Is it really out of or into my hat that the members of the board imagined I jack my limitless pun power? I'm reminded of an exchange I once witnessed. The woman tried to shock her man by extolling Jean Genet's sex practice with a pistol. But he only declared his surprise that Mr. Genet was able to stick his dick up the barrel.

CONTENTS

The SPECTRE Trilogy	12
Accidie: To Be or Not to Be	17
Klein, Hamlet & Lacan	27
One in All & All in One: Sibling, Mother & Son	33
Between Hamburg's Good Clean Fun & Vienna's Depletion: The Transvestite in Berlin	39
He's No Drag, He's My Brother: Sibling Bonds	43
Klein's Case of Hans & the School Ground of Childhood Symptoms	48
The Depressive Position	56
Trial Runs of the Mastermind	62
Therapy License	68
Hamlet's Ghosts: Jacques Derrida, Carl Schmitt, Alexander & Margaret Mitscherlich & Friedrich Jürgenson	73
From Maternal Blob to Wound Woman	84
Love-Death at the Border to the Death Wish	94
Denial & Vengeful Ghosts	99
Security Service	104
Only the Lonely	108
Caspar, Hamlet & Hans	113
Notes	119
References	125

THE SPECTRE TRILOGY

In the world of James Bond, SPECTRE is the acronym for a mouthful of vengefulness: Special Executive for Counterintelligence, Terrorism, Revenge, and Extortion. But since it doesn't quite add up, what in fact occupies the foreground is the ghostly word SPECTRE. In Ian Fleming's *Thunderball*, for example, those secretly involved in the organization bearing an acronym that retains the first word's first two letters to spell SPECTRE seem unprepared to encounter their identifying name as a word in the mix of everyday meaning and metaphor. Bond tests Largo with what he considers "an association of words": "'When I came to the table I saw a spectre.' He said the word casually, with no hint at double meaning" (143). Largo has to slap his face back on and ask Bond what he means. "Bond said lightly, 'The spectre of defeat. I thought your luck was on the turn'" (144). Largo counters with bravado:

> "My friend wishes to put the evil eye upon my cards. We have a way to deal with that where I come from." He lifted a hand, and with only the first and little fingers outstretched in a fork, he prodded once, like a snake striking toward Bond's face . . . Bond laughed good-naturedly. "That certainly put the hex on me. But what did it do to the cards? Come on, your spectre against my spectre!" (144)

After he wins three hands down, Bond once more won't give it a rest. He orders champagne and caviar for three. "'My spectre also deserves his reward.' Wondering again whether the shadow that flickered in Largo's eyes at the word had more significance than Italian superstition, he got up and followed the girl between the crowded tables to the supper room" (145-46). Bond is able to utter SPECTRE in the mix of metaphor. On the other side of the game, however, his antagonist is in demetaphorized thrall to its underworld significance or organization. And while Largo interprets Bond's spectre as an infernal demon, Bond reserves the right to choose between infernal spectres and the friendly ghosts of unfinished business (to whom consideration is owed).

Thunderball was rehearsed as Fleming's first attempt at screenplay composition. It turned into a cumulative and collaborative effort. When a certain Kevin McClory discovered that Fleming had walked away from the teamwork to write "his" novel *Thunderball*, he charged Fleming with plagiarism—which, psychoanalytically, amounts to a form of (a forum for) improper or incomplete burial. The main issue was the first appearance of SPECTRE in Fleming's writing. This third-party organization, which holds together the screen versions of *Dr. No* (1962) and *From Russia with Love* (1963) but is without mention in those novels, is in every sense a haunting projection that Fleming sought to reclaim, own up to, or release at the end of his career.[1]

Because the legal complications that had surrounded *Thunderball* deferred implementation of that made-for-the-screen work, *Dr. No* was the first Bond novel to hit the screen.[2] In the novel *From Russia with Love*, where the opposing force of evil is the Soviet organization SMERSH, Bond's assignment is to get hold of a Russian cipher machine clearly modeled after the Nazi German Enigma: the novel calls the machine "Spektor" (the screen version says "Lektor"). When Bond's boss M. extols the plan as "the most important coup that's come our way since the war" (105), he lets slip what remains most alive, even as dead, in the Cold War setting of Fleming's narratives. A close look at the novels shows that the recent past just before the Cold War presses all over the place in the details. In addition to a number of recycled Nazis, the enemy organizations that Bond must battle include leaders whose menace is hard to identify and whose German surnames could double as so-called German-Jewish names: Blofeld and Goldfinger (the latter of whom, in the book, goes by just Gold when he is alone with his gangster cohorts going for the Fort Knox gold) are just two examples. Consider the dossier on the leader of the communist underworld in Fleming's first novel, *Casino Royale*. His name, Le Chiffre, was adopted to go with the passport number that he in a sense became when, while registering as a displaced person at the end of WWII, his amnesia didn't lift. With his only recorded origin (in June 1945) being "inmate of Dachau DP camp in the US Zone of Germany," this man is given a close description in search of broader origins: "Ears small, with large lobes, indicating some Jewish blood. . . . Racially, subject is probably a mixture of Mediterranean with Prussian or Polish strains" (17).³

As a freelance third-party operation that manipulates the conflict between East and West to obtain benefits of its own, SPECTRE houses this crowd (of ghosts) while also setting the father's place. Ian Fleming's father, Valentine Fleming, was killed in May 1917 fighting the Germans. Toward the end of his career as the author of James Bond narratives—and thus in the close quarters he gave himself with SPECTRE for making reclamations and reparations—Fleming compiled and published "a tour guide in thirteen chapters for the adventurous" titled *Thrilling Cities*. Toward the close of the Berlin entry, Fleming jumps the gun in a slip (or typo) that identifies with the enemy: "From this grim capital went forth the orders that in 1916 killed my father and in 1940 my youngest brother" (141-42). Hence Ian Fleming makes a date for his father within a range of German planning and issuing of orders, which doubles as the span of the death wish. That only the first date is tampered with shows that both father and brother are in it together, with the relationship to the father appropriately bearing the brunt of murderously mixed feelings.

Once we arrive in Vienna, Fleming, in the role of tour guide, turns up the contrast of this city he dislikes to recall with the Tyrol, where he lived with substitute parental guidance following his father's death. "I learned German in the Tyrol from Mr. Ernan Forbes Dennis," who was a student "of the great psychologist Alfred Adler . . . and I learned far more about life from Ernan than from all my schooling put together" (148-49). The Tyrolese even ended up remaining Fleming's "favorite people in the world" (149). Through Adler, Fleming gained entry to greater psychoanalysis, the whole diverging spread of all that took its departure from Freud's science. "I remember in the days before the war, reading [the works] . . . of those bizarre psychologists Weininger and Groddeck—let alone the writings of Adler and Freud" (ibid).⁴

According to *Thrilling Cities*, Vienna in 1959 displays an utter lack of the intellectual and cultural activity that had defined the city (like Berlin and Munich, too) before the war (or Hitler's rule). Fleming attributes all these shortfalls to the absence of the "Jews who . . . create an atmosphere in which the intellect appears to flourish astonishingly" (149).[5] At Blofeld's introduction as the mastermind behind SPECTRE in *Thunderball*, we learn that his charisma is of the same unbounded kind that alone explains how Hitler could have enthralled "the most gifted nation in Europe" (40). From the German perspective of his identification, Fleming looks across a centuries-long generation of intelligent life—both Jewish and Gentile, both émigré and silent majority—that was utterly lost without the backup of proper succession or substitution for a long time to come.[6] This circumscribed Germany-centric framing of the view to a killing belongs among the conditions for the existence of SPECTRE. If the recent past as an introject inside SPECTRE appears in some instances to be an amalgamation of persecutors with their victims, then we must conclude that, in the traumatic era from which Fleming initially derives the Bond, there is no room for sentiment: the denizens of SPECTRE are shaken, not stirred.

In 1950, Melanie Klein relied on the literary example of Julien Green's *If I Were You*, a fable about the infernal magic of body switching, to introduce her new concept of projective identification. It's possible to turn to Ian Fleming's James Bond novels as another contemporary readymade, this time for illumination of Klein's understanding of mourning and haunting. In her 1940 essay, "Mourning and Its Relation to Manic-Depressive States," Klein introduced the notion of the "inner world" as that repository of object-identifications which mediates our contact with loss. The inner world can be seen as a modified version of melancholic incorporation, one that applies to every mourning process. The first strike of loss shakes the inner world at its foundations. The work of mourning from the outset consists in re-securing the inner world, even re-incorporating the objects that were, prior to impact, already inside its safe haven. For Fleming, it was SPECTRE, the underworld of a missing era, through which he routed his work of reparation. And SPECTRE continued, under many other names, to be a stowaway in every attempt to restart the James Bond film franchise. The underlying meaning of SPECTRE serves, even by its very persistence, as an allegory for Klein's understanding of the inner world between haunting and mourning.

The organization Fleming projected belonged to the Cold War's recent past, specifically the era of Nazi Germany, but reconfigured beyond the specifics of the former opposition, as befits a true underworld. Fleming could mix this constituency out of his own ambivalence regarding the fathers he lost and gained through "Germany." But SPECTRE also touched on larger postwar realities often obscured by denial. The mixing of perpetrators and victims in the case of SPECTRE's inner world is the kind of messy side effect that follows upon the onset of integration. Integration, a term and notion that Klein introduced into the lexicon of psychoanalytic theory in her essay on mourning, is not to be confused with or limited to the positive inclusion of elements of opposition and their adaptation to a greater whole. In Klein's conception, integration pulls up short before the prospect of irretrievable loss and includes this shortfall or incompletion in its structure. Just as the related effort of reparation cannot neutralize or deny the scene of destruction, so integration cannot circumvent or cleanse the untenable comparisons that find juxtaposition in the wake and shakeup of trauma. Out of the turbulence that integration introduces and works through, the impasse of traumatic history shifts toward the onset of the ability to mourn.

Contemporaneity is the signature of every Bond film, although each time engineered "anew." This commemorates Fleming's own hard-won ability (asserted in time for the transfer to film) to mix it up with the uninvited leftovers of the recent past. It is by the mourning work of integration that history itself becomes contemporary. Fleming's SPECTRE was not the only advance preview of integration's ongoing process, which moreover has its own history and gathering momentum. The mythic-poetic dissemination of the charge against "von Braun" and the flattening of its affect in Jean-Luc Godard's *Alphaville* (1965) takes the significance of SPECTRE out of hiding (as does the actual von Braun's pained response to his film portrayal). At the same time as Fleming projected spectral integration, Fritz Lang deflected the sentencing of opposition by the force of his Dr. Mabuse underworld. In his final film, *The 1000 Eyes of Dr. Mabuse* (1960), Lang reclaimed his earlier Dr. Mabuse films as a testimony inadmissible before Siegfried Kracauer's court of film history. That no one gets out of Dr. Mabuse's underworld alive also means that it keeps its denizens undead or alive.

ACCIDIE:
TO BE OR NOT TO BE

Fleming's decision, comparatively late in life, to marry because he was expecting fatherhood coincides with the onset of his authorship of Bond. It was 1952 and he was already in some phase of retirement from his former life in and around the UK, spending the winter months in his home in Jamaica, where he would compose each of his Bond narratives. It was to bind his anxieties about the family complex he was entering (or returning to) that Fleming started typing the first sentences of the first Bond novel from which all the rest would follow:

> The scent and smoke and sweat of a casino are nauseating at three in the morning. Then the soul-erosion produced by high gambling—a compost of greed and fear and nervous tension—becomes unbearable, and the senses awake and revolt from it. James Bond suddenly knew that he was tired. He always knew when his body or his mind had had enough, and he always acted on the knowledge. This helped him to avoid staleness and the sensual bluntness that breeds mistakes.

At this opener we already have two or more settings juxtaposed: there is the den of iniquity that shakes up (as a brink of exhaustion) equal parts Christian soul care and secular concern for nerves or psyche. But then we switch to a body or mind maintenance program that prompted the first critical reader of Fleming's novels, Fausto Antonini, to identify Bond as the new cybernetic hero, a clean and mean machine whose relationship to his interiority is covered by the double-0 icon, which in certain countries signified the public restroom. Keep it flushed! This is the aspect of the Bond that will give way in its purity before the emergence of SPECTRE from the initial juxtaposition of settings of spiritual and psychic exhaustion.

Married with child, Fleming became the author of spy thrillers that drew on his wartime work for British intelligence but were engaged in the Cold War, the native habitat of their genre. His literary day job was with *The Sunday Times*. Fleming proposed a series of reflections on the Seven Deadly Sins by seven distinguished authors to appear in *The Times*. In the foreword to their subsequent collection as a book of essays, Fleming slides into the James Bond mode of worldliness and gives us the stiff upper flip-off that the original seven sins are by now outmoded, replaced by new and improved sins—with one exception, which also belongs to the world of the Bond: "Of all the seven, only Sloth in its extreme form of *accidia*, which is a form of spiritual suicide and a refusal of joy, . . . has my wholehearted condemnation, perhaps because in moments of despair I have seen its face" (ix).

In *You Only Live Twice*, the novel in which SPECTRE is busted or put to rest, Blofeld looks back on his thwarted attempts to be kind through threatened cruelty. In *Thunderball*, he sought to extort great sums of money in exchange for the atomic missiles he had stolen and was prepared to detonate in selective locations. But he was also providing work of caution that would have prepared the world to adopt the necessary defensive and preventive measures in the face of inevitable rogue appropriation and deployment of weapons of mass destruction. His next scheme, in *On Her Majesty's Secret Service*, the open declaration of bacteriological war against Britain if funds weren't forthcoming, might have forced the people he was threatening out of "lethargy into the kind of community effort we witnessed during the war" (145). This third time around, Blofeld has set up a "Castle of Death" in Japan, its gardens stocked with poisonous plants and lethal reptiles and insects, allegedly for research purposes. But the fortifications and the shark-infested moat, like the large signs prohibiting trespass, instead advertise to countless persons seeking death the true garden of ending it. This time Blofeld is neither committing nor threatening any overt crime. His inadvertent service at first sight is to offer a more efficient means of disposal for the suicidally inclined. But once paid off to move away, which is the goal of his implicit blackmailing of the Japanese government, Japan will have been taught a lessening of the cultural valorization of suicide as an honorable way out. In this final incarnation of SPECTRE—for which Blofeld no longer needs its name or allegorical caption—the mastermind has taken up residence in the close quarters of the deferral of his own suicidality:

> I will make a confession to you, Mister Bond. I have come to suffer from a certain lassitude of mind which I am determined to combat. This comes in part from being a unique genius who is alone in the world, without honor—worse, misunderstood. No doubt much of the root cause of this accidie is physical—liver, kidneys, heart, the usual weak points of the middle-aged. But there has developed in me a certain mental lameness, a disinterest in humanity and its future, an utter boredom with the affairs of mankind. (146)

In Fleming's *Thunderball*, Bond was the last to believe in the existence of SPECTRE as a third party to world conflict rather than, for example, just another front for Cold War hostilities. In the next novel, *On Her Majesty's Secret Service*, Bond is already one year into the assignment he was given to confirm that SPECTRE was in fact dismantled. Because he has all along been convinced that there was nothing left for him to keep after, find, or lose, he has determined to submit his resignation from the service at the start of the novel, since he appears to have been in effect relieved of his double-0 duties. When Fleming launched the Bond series in 1953, he set the superhero at an age and in a condition of health that would qualify him for retirement in another ten years or so. Fleming was on this schedule, too, when it comes to Bond's relationship with SPECTRE.

Before Fleming begins opening up the adult profile of mourning or depression in Bond, he sets the novel going with Bond's involuntary memories of early childhood by the sea. According to the history Fleming took down of Bond, the agent licensed to kill lost both parents, casualties of a climbing accident, when he was twelve years old. "It was all there, his own childhood, spread out before him to have another look at" (10). But after two more sentences immersed in time's passage, Bond, fast on the inoculative intake, pulls the emergency chain: "Impatiently Bond lit a cigarette, pulled his shoulders out of their slouch and slammed the mawkish memories back into their long-closed file" (ibid.). At the same time, he is keeping watch over his last night stand, Tracy, who is again contemplating suicide according to the terms of the contract with her dead child, which she has taken out on herself. By the end of the novel, Bond's intervention will lead to their union in matrimony, following her stint in a Swiss asylum where she works through her grief. To get to this point, Bond too must work through the pre-Oedipal plotting of SPECTRE via girls from the UK Blofeld regresses to infancy for post-hypnotic suggestion. Though Bond succeeds in destroying the SPECTRE operation Blofeld restored after his defeat in *Thunderball*, Blofeld himself, now referred to as the "Big One" (182), gets away. In the wake of this getaway, Tracy calls Bond back to the onset of responsibilities:

> "You don't seem to think it matters to anyone. The way you go on playing Red Indians. It's so—so selfish."
> Bond reached out and pressed her hand on the wheel. He hated "scenes." But it was true what she said. . . . It never crossed his mind that anybody really cared about him. . . . But now, in three days' time, he would no longer be alone. He would be a half of two people. . . . Now, if he got himself killed, there would be Tracy who would at any rate partially die with him. (180-81)

That Bond is only playing Red Indians is the disparagement of his agency with which his antagonists regularly taunt him on the wavelength, as we know from his bouts of self-recrimination, of Bond's own superego. Dr. Shatterhand, the pseudonym Blofeld will assume in the next novel, *You Only Live Twice*, is the old citation or introject of "playing Red Indians" in the German-language world. Alongside Winnetou, the Indian chief object of identification, Karl May introduced his good white friend and ally, Old Shatterhand. Thus the Germanic niche or crypt of Fleming's parental bond of couplification and mourning—the shattering of the "and"—continues to summon Bond's special agency for final reckonings.

While Mr. and Mrs. Bond drive to their wedding night, Blofeld and Irma Bunt, revealed in this parting shot for the first time as the other couple, drive-by shoot Bond's partner in couplification and successful mourning. Just prior to this conclusion, Bond had extolled to Tracy the main attraction of their first stopover, Kufstein, in the Tyrol: "Bond put his mouth up close to Tracy's ear and told her about . . . the most imaginative war memorial, for the 1914-18 war, ever devised. Punctually at midday every day, the windows of the castle are thrown open and a voluntary is played on the great organ inside" (189).

As introduced in *Thunderball*, SPECTRE was Blofeld's first underworld organization employing living agents, former assassins and spies of various secret service outfits and representatives of the world's leading criminal organizations. Before SPECTRE, Blofeld incorporated himself as a series of organizations comprised of what he sold to all sides of world conflict: stolen information. Though it seemed a downgrade coming out of a highly successful course of university studies, he carefully selected his first position in the Polish Ministry of Posts and Telegraphs because he "had decided that fast and accurate communication lay, in a contracting world, at the very heart of power" (41). Collecting information crossing the wires of this power at his desk, he also began to steal the identifying data of persons he would never meet, but with whose "identities" he could simulate large intelligence operations. Blofeld sets up SPECTRE as a finite project for raising funds that will allow him to retire from his insider speculations on politics and psychosis.

What SPECTRE asks for tends not to exceed what any ghost (according to countless stories and manuals) might be expected to request in the fixated effort to bring something in extended lifetime to closure. This becomes ever clearer the more deeply we enter the era of Bond's projection. In the 1969 film *On Her Majesty's Secret Service*, Blofeld threatens to inflict instant infertility on countless life forms, a threat that he at least never expects to carry out. In exchange for withdrawal of a fantastically apocalyptic threat, Blofeld wants amnesty—in other words, a new release of life out of hiding or incarceration—and recognition of his claim to a noble title. In psychodynamic terms, he wishes to look for love among his good internal objects, whose fundamental contribution to his makeup, however, it is up to the world powers to recognize. Total world domination thus has an internal spin as one of SPECTRE's transitional objectives.

The novel *You Only Live Twice* already in its title reverses and preserves the ghost logic of mourning according to which you only die twice. Hence the novel commences as therapy for Bond. Sir James Molony, the neurologist attached to the Secret Service, who was awarded the Nobel Prize for his Adlerian titled study *Some Psychosomatic Side-effects of Organic Inferiority*, counsels M. to find for his special agent a mission impossible that would inject upward mobilization into his grief-stuck metabolism. "I don't mean necessarily dangerous, like assassination or stealing Russian cyphers or whatever. But something that's desperately important but apparently impossible" (19).

Because Dr. Shatterhand's research establishment is strictly legal, but also because the Japanese are paralyzed before their biggest symptom—in which they cannot intervene because it is the open invitational they already occupy or cathect—Bond is offered as rescuer in exchange for Japanese cooperation with Britain's efforts to restore the crumbling range of influence of its Secret Service. His host in Japan, Tanaka, initiates Bond into Japanese culture as the refined gathering of senses and verities immersed in finitude. His appointment to this task comes out of the mix of his heritages: educated in the UK, Tanaka nevertheless took the side of his place of birth in WWII all the way to the inside of preparedness for the kamikaze defense. The success or significance of Bond's assignment, which requires that he go undercover, depends on Bond's assumption of a Japanese identity and identification. But the closest fit of the cover will prove to be an identification at cross-purposes that stays with death or suicide and stops short of the dead. As Tanaka extols the virtues of Kamikaze suicide, Bond identifies more with Tanaka's trance state than with its content: "Tiger was completely sent. He was back there again fighting the war. Bond knew the symptoms. He often visited this haunted forest of memory himself" (74). Bond will take his departure from Tiger's readiness for death by adding the relationship to identifiable objects, lost and found, to this generalized haunting.

In what amounts to their last prep session on the way to the location of Bond's assignment, several breakthroughs take place. The day begins with a visit to Japan's oldest brothel, which, now that prostitution is illegal, remains open as an historical monument. Bond asks how many bedrooms there are. Only four. "That's no way to run a whore-house. . . . You need quick through-put, like a casino" (84). Bond, Tanaka says, has missed the point. "In former times, this was a place of rest and recreation. Food was served and there was music and story-telling. People would write *tankas*. Take that inscription on the wall. It says, 'Everything is new tomorrow.' Some man with a profound mind will have written that" (ibid.). Some man whose own name subsumes the *tanka* genre cites or summons the very limits of the novel subsuming him. Some man will have written the *tanka* that is the quintessential Fleming sentence which the post-Fleming titles of Bond films, like *Tomorrow Never Dies* (1997), will struggle to duplicate or parody. Sure, Bond replies. But then someone would interrupt the proceedings, reach for his sword, and demand one of the four occupied bedrooms. Bond's resistance takes the form of prosecuting certain claims to sublimation for the repression driving the stakes. It nevertheless crosses over into the kind of intervention that presupposes identification: "Everyone tries to forget his rowdy past instead of being proud of it" (ibid.). Then he concludes by overstepping his intervention and setting himself up for the backfire of breakthrough: "You shouldn't try and pretend that your oldest whore-house is a sort of Stratford-on-Avon." We are at the point of crossing over.

The next round of literary chitchat shows Bond's ignorance of a certain seventeenth-century *haiku* poet. Tanaka is prompted to summon as many big names of Western literature as would fit into a hand of cards to bear witness to the enormity of this loss. Given out of chronological order, the shelf life of western civilization is propped up by two bookends: Shakespeare and Goethe (85). Bond tries to be accommodating, but he cannot accept Tanaka's claim, based on several samples, that the unknown poet is Shakespeare's equal. Tanaka just the same suggests that, if Bond is to enter into an understanding of the *haiku*, he must try to compose one of his own. The result is Bond's authorship of the title of Fleming's narrative:

> You only live twice:
> Once when you're born,
> And once when you look death in the face. (86)

Tanaka is delighted with what he considers a breakthrough: a sincere effort that reflects on the mission.

It is not until they check into the local police station, built in the yellow-brick German style of the Axis era (93), that the breakthrough in fact occurs, one that exceeds the Kamikaze therapy that aims at looking one's own death in the face. Bond's dead are now in his face. While looking over surveillance shots of Dr. Shatterhand's castle, Bond recognizes who's in this Dracula castle for keeps: Blofeld and Irma Bunt (97), the couple that is SPECTRE, now the ghost of his own couple's past, both his missing marriage and the couple of parents.

He won't tell Tanaka who Dr. Shatterhand is (98). That would take the case out of his hands. The photographic evidence transmits to him the summons for revenge. Remember me.

Prior to arrival at the police station, at the point of crossing over in their literary work of identification, Bond and Tanaka breakfasted on ham omelets called "Hamlets" (85). And as he prepares under double cover in the fishing village to launch his covert operations against the Castle of Death, Bond learns that the locals refer to Dr. Shatterhand as a foreign body: both "the devil himself" and "the incarnation of all the evil in the West" (114). But local customs and shrines tend to make room for ghosts, many of them "friendly" (116). After a night of dreaming "of ghosts and demons," Bond encounters Blofeld on this questionable ground. "And so, Mister Bond, I came to devise this useful and essentially humane project—the offer of free death to those who seek release from the burden of being alive. By doing so, I have . . . provided the common man with a solution to the problem of whether to be or not to be" (146).

SPECTRE appears at the juncture of questioning where Hamlet encounters his specter. Is the ghost of his father the dead father doing the limbo because he has unfinished business to entrust to his son? Or is he a demon sent from hell? The infernal relation is never seriously pursued. But there is yet another question that is never raised as such. Hamlet acts it out as his famous procrastination: what is the identity of or the identification with the ghost? Put differently: has there been a murder or is not the ghost of the father the strong sign that mourning is disturbed, interrupted, abbreviated, and thus too successful by half, the vengeful violent half? Isn't murder in Shakespeare's play what successful mourning and ready substitution inflict upon the dead? There is the death of the other, but then there's the second death, which is murder.

In *Hamlet*, there's no reason to trust the paternal ghost who is otherwise the master of ceremonies at the pageant of second death. The secular mind was catching up with the goods of this world, which, since hardly good enough in comparison with what awaits us in the other world, were consigned in the Christian era to the trash heap of waiting around, or otherwise stored under projective layers of evil and demonization. Marlowe's Doctor Faustus steps up to the plate—"Sweet Mephistophilis!"—and, during the twenty-four year (or hour) span of deathless consuming-time, he gets to know the world of his own making. The medium for his striving is magic, a good catchall for everything Christianity excluded and prosecuted. The world opens wide to him via magic. As a secular subject, Faustus accepts the Devil's best offer, a finite span of quality time and then the deadline. He translates Hell with Elysium or with this world, and Christian Devils with pagan daemons or spirits of the dead. But once he binds himself to the most powerful Devil magic can provide, Faustus must endure the sermonizing shine Mephistophilis takes to Christianity. The problem Faustus faces at, or as, the end is that he cannot be certain that there is a time limit to his death or afterlife. He knows that human striving, knowing, and consuming cannot be reduced to lifetime. His necromantic overskill push-buttons ghosts around as his agents of long-distance travel and communication. Faustus does not want to slave as a ghost for the next in line with an owner's manual. Focusing always only on his own death and life, Faustus must look forward to his own ghostliness as so abhorrent that it might as well be Hell. Uninhibited by Christianity, Faustus gets his groove back. But he gets his grave back, too.

With Shakespeare's Hamlet, we get to know the ghosts as the detour to self-knowledge missing from Faustus's more direct and less protected hit of what's worth knowing. In *Hamlet*, the second death or life is thus subsumed by mourning, which in turn can be seen to replace the magic so central to *The Tragical History of Doctor Faustus* as the main medium for reopening the stage of the world following the withdrawal of Christianity's dominion. As was the case with magic in *Doctor Faustus*, the medium of mourning in *Hamlet* still includes fragments of the former Christian hierarchy as coordinates for steering the course of ghost communication and ghost-making. The ghost of Hamlet's father explains his in-between state and schedule by the timing of his death: without a time-out for absolution, he went down in the midst of his worldly life sans ethical cleansing. Hamlet spares Claudius because he finds him at prayer—a ready position to let his soul fly straight to Heaven and escape the full weight (and waiting around) of revenge. Doctor Faustus issues his ultimate affirmation of the secular world and word in his embrace of Helen of Troy. This first ending of Marlowe's tragical history, which the second ending takes back again, was where Goethe picked up *Hamlet* to steer his Faust clear of Christian doom to rescue. Too briefly, Marlowe's Faustus proclaims that his world is let go and recycled via Helen, and that all that is not Helen is what some still call Hell. At the end of Goethe's *Faust*, unstoppable mourning—the eternal or internal feminine—stays the "and" between Helen and Hell, Elysium and Heaven, and cheats the Faustian deferral of suicide of its infernal punch line.

KLEIN, HAMLET & LACAN

Something old and something new has to be juxtaposed to read Bond as a superhero with a license to kill. To the extent that she directly addressed the mortal sins Greed and Envy as metabolization phases of an inner world of our own making, which is basically spectral, Melanie Klein's oeuvre overlaps with Fleming's frame of reference. We are considering this frame of reference as Elizabethan because it is as Christian as it is secular or deregulated. The first time we see his face, behind closed doors in *Thunderball*, Blofeld is already marked or marred by this oversize identification: "Only the mouth, under a heavy, squat nose, marred what might have been the face of a philosopher or a scientist. Proud and thin, like a badly healed wound, the compressed, dark lips, capable only of false, ugly smiles, suggested contempt, tyranny, and cruelty—but to an almost Shakespearian degree" (44).

Although Alfred Adler explicitly thematized Nietzschean notions within the lexicon of greater psychoanalysis, Klein offers a wider and more differentiating opening for Nietzsche-through-Freud transmissions in the course of her theorization of early splitting between the good and bad breasts.

At first, the good breast alone counts; the bad or absent breast is a throwaway afterthought. But no one can leave good enough alone. The good object, as the focus and frontier of reality, is subjected to all of little one's testing protocols; it is devoured, controlled, opened wide, explored, its inner creative goods taken out, away, and in. Anxiety follows at the prospect of the object's retaliation. Splitting proper between good and bad breasts (and objects) commences, largely via internalization, as a defense against anxiety. Now there is or will be an inner world. What drives the splitting—as a process that can result, the infant foresees, in the good object's utter destruction—is evil.

Klein's unique valorization of idealization is the intervention to follow for distinguishing between infantile morality and its ambivalent, Oedipal complexification. The distinction appears untenable within the retrospective of regression. In real time, however, infancy (i.e., pre-regression) admits not only separation of good and bad. It also admits an idealization of the good as inexhaustible together with a protective denial of the very existence of the bad. The denial is made possible by strong feelings of omnipotence. This establishment of the good of this world is immediately reversed in the unconscious through the death drive and its reintroduction of relationality under the aegis of annihilation.

Over time, what administers the different tide or time charts of early development as positions or juxtapositions is mourning as the reinstatement of the inner world of objects. In the beginning, states of disintegration are mitigated by contact with the external good object. That object exists or you're dead. But later on there are no guarantees that good objects exist for you in the external world. The reversal of values picks up the lack: the bad comes to be treated as good enough, while omnipotence must be viewed as evil, as annihilating. My bad cannot become my evil. The good cannot be let go. We are all poorly constituted on impact with the loss of a loved one. The mourner, who must prove good enough, is linked to the lost good object via the evil of annihilation. The object is gone for good. In struggling to reverse or contain this evil, contact with the good can be maintained. Hence loss as annihilation is, for Klein, the manifestation of the Death Drive. And while she closes Freud's distance as devil's advocate to the Death Drive, she makes the Devil, as prince or principle of evil annihilation, subservient to the spectral metabolization of the inner world. Once the internal world is in place, what comes or doesn't come our way can be brought before the internal good object to be borne.

Serious knowledge of Klein's work would appear restricted to clinicians. And yet, as point of reference, Klein was key to mapping the philosophical reception of psychoanalysis. Both Michel Foucault and Gilles Deleuze surveyed psychoanalysis as extending through two post-Freudian figures, Jacques Lacan and Klein. The reception of Lacan's thought would tend to subsume Klein as imaginary to the Lacanian symbolic. But it is over the issue of mourning that this fork in the future of Freud's science can be read otherwise.

Lacan raised his bar by lifting Klein's 1940 essay, "Mourning and Its Relation to Manic-Depressive States," up inside the symbolic grid alongside *Hamlet*. In "Desire and the Interpretation of Desire in *Hamlet*," Lacan, the analyst who avoided mourning and melancholia like a pest, finds that he alone recognizes that in *Hamlet* "all anyone talks about is mourning" (39). Phantoms arise because mourning rites have been curtailed or otherwise improperly carried out. The ritual value of mourning refers to and summons a "total mass intervention, from the heights of heaven to the depths of hell, of the entire play of the symbolic register" (38). While the inside view of the symbolic register in its entirety as still home on the range of Christianity doesn't fit the Elizabethan frame, Lacan does admit that, while only the totality of the signifier can fill or fulfill the hole in the real, we are faced in mourning with the "inadequacy of signifying elements to cope with the hole." Just as mourning must mediate a strike of loss that threatens the inner world in Klein's essay, so in Lacan's reading of mourning in *Hamlet*, "the system of signifiers in their totality . . . is impeached by the least instance of mourning" (38). That's why the rites of mourning realign the gap opened up by a direct hit of absence with the greater gap that is always also there, "the symbolic lack." What does it mean that every encounter with the loss of a loved one constitutes a renewal of vows of substitution with the separations and sacrifices already given at the office of Oedipus by following the complex into its decline? If he rids his reading of the loss of all singularity, then Lacan overshoots Klein's mark, the inner world.

When he slides aberrant mourning into Freud's "The Decline of the Oedipus Complex," Lacan finds in this vicinity a certain association between latency and lassitude, thereby summoning the Elizabethan frame of reference of mortal sins as Christianity leftovers marking stations of psychic metabolism. Prompted by *Hamlet*, Lacan stumbles over the underworld trajectory in Freud, a bypass operation that skips but preserves the heart of the matter of Hamlet as first neurotic with an Oedipus Complex. Freud extends his use of latency in *Moses and Monotheism*, the work where he openly settled with his specter in a multiple setting of upheaval to which the speculative work stood in an inoculative or latent relationship. Behind Freud's specter stands a foreign body in the place of the father. The transference, as Freud immediately recognized, is the demo specter in everyone's life proving the reality or staying power of identifiable losses. In Freud's case, the transfer on the way to the settlement of his paternal history conveyed in the beginning a lost child, his infant brother Julius, to the onset of undercover operations.[7]

Freud's and Klein's attributions of reality testing to the work of mourning press toward the encounter with the specter. According to Freud, the mourner is compelled to submit the continuity shots of the departed to reality checks. Lacan translates this into his symbolic grid as the psychosis-like profusion of images rushing to fill the gap in the real. The consequence of Freud's decision to fill out a missing person report in consideration of mourning—both Klein and Lacan note that Freud was the first to assign an object to mourning—is in turn lost if we view Freud's introduction of reality testing in his 1917 essay "Mourning and Melancholia" as exclusively in the disposal service of successful mourning. Klein opens her mourning essay with three citations from "Mourning and Melancholia" in which Freud addresses reality testing. The third time, it's the harm apparently done by Freud's passage on reality's verdict decreeing the object's non-existence that alerts us to the closeness of Klein's reading based on Freud's collected work. Freud states that he does not know if this is in fact so but that "possibly" the survivor lets the lost object go, satisfied with the prospect of living on. But the letting go of the goner is possibly possible only because, over the time of mourning, the requisite expenditure of energy has dissipated and the task is more easily done than said. As Klein shows, Freud's closing words could also signify that the time of mourning undoes the initial period at the end of the death sentence handed down to the survivor according to which he must choose either to let the dead go or to join them. In the time of mourning, then, Klein situates reality testing as the séance of communication that unites living and dead objects against direct hits of loss.

Lacan, like Klein in her essay, does not address mourning at first contact, but in the suffer zone of generic loss. Only an investment, mourning is locked into the scheme of development, which, for Klein, is modeled by early experiences of loss of the breast, the first cut that cuts deepest. Lacan translates this into mourning for the phallus. In Lacan's case, the mourning double-take must also swerve from the ghost on the same page he is on with his reading assignment. The phantom is the phallus that can't be struck down or mourned. Only when ready to die oneself—to immerse oneself in the mass-suicidal twilight of the gods—can one strike this phantom or phallus.

The contrast between them is that Klein addresses ghosts and only ghosts, though never by name in her essay on mourning. What Freud did for mourning or unmourning, namely fix the focus on the object relationship, Klein did for the inner world of identifications, which are similarly embodied and personified as object relations. Already the infant builds the internal world through a friendly cannibalism of the parents. Despite being altered by the infant's own phantasms and impulses, the opening installation of the inner world still corresponds to actual experiences and impressions gained from the external world. Unpleasant experiences out there cause reality testing to turn inward. In the face of dangers, the child senses that he can retain or re-attain his objects as well as their love for him and his love for them, preserving or re-establishing the internal good life. Enjoyable experiences are equally necessary though differently applied: they are the proofs that loved objects inside as well as outside are not injured, are safe, are not turning vengeful. If the living is easy and love and trust increase, then the baby is able "to test his inner reality by means of outer reality" (347).

Freud argues that the mourner reinstates the lost object inside the ego. Klein adds: "In my view, however, he not only takes into himself (reincorporates) the person whom he has just lost, but also reinstates his internalised good objects" (353). Mourning means for Klein, in the first place, to "rebuild with anguish the inner world, which is felt to be in danger of deteriorating and collapsing" (354). After a considerable delay, the 1940 mourning essay was Klein's own more direct response to the mysterious death of her son Hans in a climbing accident. Hans's death (rumored to have been suicide) caused sister Melitta Schmideberg to break once and for all with their mother, whom she blamed for her brother's death. In the essay, the case of Mrs. A is the case of Mrs. Klein twice over. That this case-example mother loses a young son who died while at school encodes Hans's earlier appearance in Klein's oeuvre—the other inner world—as Felix (e.g., in the 1925 essay "A Contribution to the Psychogenesis of Tics").

In 1940, through a relay of dreams, the grief-stuck mother revisits early death wishes addressed to a mother and son who were identifiable only by dint of having once been resented by her brother and mother, both long dead. The dream thought announced that the unpleasant woman's son, who hurt her brother and mother, should die. But what transmits between these lines is: my mother's son died, not my own. A contrasting feeling was at the same time struck up: sympathy with her mother and thus sorrow for herself. Her mother should not lose her grandson, too. Grief goes to or through the internalized mother, who suffers together with her. "The tears which she shed were also to some extent the tears which her internal parents shed, and she also wanted to comfort them as they—in her phantasy—comforted her" (359). Reincorporation of the internal objects catches up with the first tendency in mourning to pull back from direct contact with loss.

Only if life inside and outside is secured as going on after all can the mourner preserve her loved object, admit him within her haunted corpus. Mourning is just one more unhappy experience that can deepen the relationship to inner objects and allow one to dig in with one's ghosts. There is even a happiness involved in regaining them after you felt they were long gone upon impact of the new identifiable loss. Mourning is not about contact with loss, except as developmentally first and, over time, repeatable. The contact person, however, joins the other identifiable ghosts in the inner sanctum, which is what the next new loss will also ultimately threaten.

ONE IN ALL & ALL IN ONE: SIBLING, MOTHER & SON

From the start, Freud set melancholia apart from the transference neuroses. Although he placed melancholia at the front of the line of the narcissistic neuroses, Freud again set it apart from more severe forms of narcissistic disturbance as, in effect, the original borderline psychosis. In my study of Philip K. Dick's oeuvre and its intertexts, I tried to explore and construct, on an endopsychic-genealogical basis, if not in fact, the ways in which melancholic encryptment leads, like a kind of spirit guide, to the stabilization, encapsulation, and legibility of otherwise extreme psychotic states (including Daniel Paul Schreber's paranoid schizophrenia).

But a distinction came to be drawn also within melancholia itself in the all-out effort to read the influence or politics of administered and treated trauma. While historical distinction is at issue,[8] it is also distinction as selection and valuation that entered the receiving area of the crypt. Strictly speaking, a true crypt carrier is not to be confused with the melancholic mouthpiece of self-recriminations (though this drag can be put on as a diversion away from the crypt's concealment). The goner enters the crypt for good. Only what is good and gone can be preserved. An occult analogy may help out here. It's true that the werewolf is the other melancholic, indeed emphatically so, since his very name (i.e., lycanthrope) issues the diagnosis of melancholic incorporation. While vampirism, in contrast, gets immersed in melancholia to flesh out the crypt it transmits and by which it is transmitted, the melancholic werewolf wallows in the death wish. That's why he invariably begs a true love to release him from his sorry state. But the vampire as crypt carrier holds the good in storage, not the bad and ugly. Though he perpetrates the wounding of the loss of the good on his chosen victims, who tend to start out as survivors of earlier victims, he also, at least always potentially, makes provision for all of them to enter the crypt. Vampirism is a selection process that goes into the crypt's foundation.

The selection process is another way of trying out or testing. After the fact, Klein's theorization of the inner world as the crux of psychic reality extends through her earlier work as a series of trial runs that sort through the ambivalence of inheritance. The mourning essay incorporates a two-paragraph-long discussion of ambivalence from Klein's 1935 essay "A Contribution to the Psychogenesis of Manic-Depressive States." The only bracketed insert within the quotation introduces and underscores "idealization" (350). This guarantees that the path not taken by Klein's mourning work is the normal path to or through ambivalence.

By turning up the contrast to the fantasy of immediate flight to the internal good objects, Klein subtly highlights the inner world's process of preservation as ongoing and highly vulnerable. She recognizes daughter Melitta Schmideberg at this point of takeoff. In her 1930 study, Schmideberg argues that "the ego takes refuge in an extravagant belief in the benevolence of his internalized objects" (288). This flight, which entails denial of psychic and external reality, lands inside the deepest psychosis. In closing, Klein gives kudos not only to her daughter for insights into paranoia but also to Freud for his understanding of ambivalence. However, the ambivalence that serves Freud as a watchword of acceptance of good and bad (within the frame of their reversal into evil and good) remains for Klein partial to the good object; it "is partly a safeguard against one's own hate and against the hated and terrifying objects" (ibid.). It is her way of saying that, for her, Freud is the good object.

In "Mourning and its Relation to Manic-Depressive States," Klein shows sorting out to be fundamental to the commitment to the inner world. When Klein's double, Mrs. A, starts sorting through her dead son's letters, she goes further than the typical tidying up of the home and rearrangement of the furniture performed by other people in mourning. The household routines carried out at the time of grief "spring from an increase of the obsessional mechanisms which are a repetition of one of the defenses used to combat the infantile depressive position" (356). The mail sorting room (through which Mrs. A's mourning passes) leads to the first in a series of dreams opening onto the modified passage between crypt and inner world.

> Mrs. A, in the first few days after the shattering loss of her young son . . . took to sorting out letters, keeping his and throwing others away. She was thus unconsciously attempting to restore him and keep him safe inside herself, and throwing out what she felt to be indifferent, or rather hostile—that is to say, the "bad" objects, dangerous excreta and bad feelings. (355-56)

Inside her essay on mourning, Klein reopens "A Contribution to the Psychogenesis of Manic-Depressive States" as at once incorporated and "modified." In mourning, the subject goes through a modified and transitory manic-depressive state and overcomes it (354). In all varieties of mourning, the depressive position is reactivated: the child goes through a "transitory manic-depressive state as well as a state of mourning" (369). These become "modified" in turn by the "infantile neurosis" (ibid.). Once this neurosis has been passed through and passes on, the depressive position, too, shall be overcome. In mourning, the revived depressive position (revived by the loss of the loved object) "becomes modified again" and is overcome in the same way the ego overcame it in childhood. The lost person is installed in the course of reinstalling the good parents.

The depressive position adds a new set of feelings and phantasies to the earlier set carried over from an earlier position (later to be named the paranoid-schizoid position) characterized by persecution and destruction of the ego by bad internal objects (348). Organized around pining for the loved good object, the new set triggers manic defenses. Omnipotent phantasies that reflect the extreme frightfulness of the persecutors and the extreme perfection of the good objects control or master the bad objects and save or restore the loved ones.

In early development, the young child doesn't have adequate means to cope. In addition to manic measures, there are also obsessional repetitive means of coping with guilt and anxiety (350). The obsessional mode, always proximate to the manic mode, also supplies an alternate way of attempting reparation. But the benign circle of reparation is broken when the desire to control the object, to triumph over it, enters with these attempts. Klein replaces the circle with a two-track approach. The actual loss dips down inside the inner world, thereby reactivating relations with one's original contact persons, who must also be rescued. Just as the very young child struggles to establish the inner world, so the mourner struggles to re-establish and reintegrate it.

What comes to pass is the infantile neurosis. When, through proofs and counter-proofs, both manic omnipotence and the obsessional mode of the reparation attempts decrease, "the infantile neurosis has passed" (353). Mourning or analysis can diminish the anxieties about persecuting internal parents. In session, "patients are enabled to revise their relation to their parents—whether they be dead or alive—and to rehabilitate them to some extent even if they have grounds for actual grievances" (369). When "greater tolerance" becomes available, good parent figures can be set up more securely alongside the bad ones while fear of the latter now comes to be mitigated by trust in the former. The full range of emotions can now be experienced—mourning can be gone through—unto the end of the infantile depressive position.

The "actual loss of a loved person" is increased by the mourner's "unconscious phantasies of having lost his *internal* 'good' objects as well" (353). If the internal bad objects predominate, then the balancing or sorting act between bad and good collapses. "The greatest danger for the mourner comes from the turning of his hatred against the loved person himself" (354). And yet hatred's turn is inevitable. A loved person who dies is immediately representative of early important figures and thus inherits the mixed feelings addressed to them. Hatred of the lost loved object not only turns the object into a persecutor but also shakes the mourner's "belief in his good inner objects" (355). Hate, especially reinforced by the sense that the loved one's dying on him was enacted as punishment, disturbs the process of idealization that allows the mourner to experience "reassurance" in "keeping his loved object for the time being as an idealized one" (ibid.). All along "the idealized mother" was the "safeguard against a retaliatory or a dead mother" and thus represented "security and life itself" (ibid.).

Mrs. A's first remembered dream in the wake of the loss of her son, which followed the male sorting between good and bad, featured a couple, a mother in black and her son, marked either as dead or going to die. While the dreamer offers condolence, she feels hostility toward the two people (356). The associations bring up an important childhood memory of her own mother's son, her older brother. Her brother as idol was toppled when difficulties in his schoolwork required tutoring by a peer. At least when the mother of the peer showed up to make the coaching arrangements, she appeared condescending, or rather Mrs. A's mother appeared dejected. Mrs. A took away from this visitation a sense of disgrace fallen upon her beloved brother and the whole family. The figures in her dream, Mrs. B and her son, were then the messengers of this disgrace. And yet the strength of her feelings about the incident reflects "her unconscious feelings of guilt" (ibid.). She identified strongly with her brother, who was openly chagrined by the situation and expressed dislike of the other boy. Hence she takes revenge upon Mrs. B and son. But there are other "very deeply repressed wishes" that also come back with the B scenario. Mrs. A loved and admired her brother. She was also jealous of him and envied his greater knowledge, his mental and physical superiority, and his possession of a penis. That she was jealous of her beloved mother for possessing such a son contributed to the triumph she experienced when her brother died. The "triumph" enters the passage of modification by first becoming "associated with control of the internalized mother and brother" (357). By spinning these controls, Mrs. A's grief was displaced from herself onto her internalized mother, kept separate via denial. It's okay if "*a* boy dies" (ibid.)—it's even satisfactory. Again, though, ambivalence is largely a safeguard for Klein against the bad influence of inimical objects. What follows, "modified through her strong motherly feelings," is her brother's passage into the inner world: "The mourning for her brother . . . entered into her present grief" over her son (ibid.). The crypt supports the rebuilding of the inner world in mourning.

In the course of calibrating the vent given to feelings of grief, it is again the sorting mechanism of the inner world, but more specifically in this case (as in Klein's case) inside the passage between crypt and inner world, that comes into play.

> It seems that the processes of projecting and ejecting, which are closely connected with giving vent to feelings, are held up in certain stages of grief by an extensive manic control, and can again operate more freely when that control relaxes. Through tears, the mourner not only expresses his feelings and thus eases tension, but, since in the unconscious they are equated with excrements, he also expels his "bad" feelings and his "bad" objects, and this adds to the relief obtained through crying. This greater freedom in the

inner world implies that the internalized objects, being less controlled by the ego, are also allowed more freedom: that these objects themselves are allowed in particular, greater freedom of feeling. In the mourner's state of mind, the feelings of his internal objects are also sorrowful. In his mind, they share his grief, in the same way as actual kind parents would. (359)

After Mrs. A has passed through the whole sequence of arrangements and rearrangements with her already good and gone internalized objects, she can now admit her current loss inside the inner world and give the new lost object shelter. "Thus while grief is experienced to the full and despair is at its height, the love for the object wells up and the mourner feels more strongly that life inside and outside will go on after all, and that the lost loved object can be preserved within" (360). Now it is by their very survival that the internal objects prove to be good and helpful.

BETWEEN HAMBURG'S GOOD CLEAN FUN & VIENNA'S DEPLETION: THE TRANSVESTITE IN BERLIN

Before closing the chapter on Berlin in his tour guide *Thrilling Cities*, Fleming releases his nightmare vision of German unstoppability, which stood behind or to the side of the version he had contemplated in *Moonraker* but hot off the repression.[9] Fleming presents his "waking nightmare" of a German techno-future that's given a third outside chance (three strikes and you're outside, on the winning side).

> In these places I have a recurrent waking nightmare: it is ten, twenty, fifty years later in the Harz Mountains, or in the depths of the Black Forest. The whole of a green and smiling field slides silently back to reveal the dark mouth of a great subterranean redoubt. With a whine of thousands of horsepower, behind a mass of brilliant machinery . . . the tip of a gigantic rocket emerges above the surrounding young green trees. England has rejected the ultimatum. First there is a thin trickle of steam from the rocket exhausts and then a great belch of flame, and slowly, very slowly, the rocket climbs off its underground launching pad. And then it is on its way. (142)

Although identified as a daymare, Fleming's vision is set not on the fantasy genre but on the recognizably occult Faustian frame, which is at once infernal and ghostly. That is why, with room for ambivalence, the momentum of return doesn't stop here. Crossing the German springtime en route to Vienna from Berlin, Fleming drives through landscapes and towns that inspire a love of Germany. In a gesture that follows in the goosesteps of a certain German recent past, Fleming imagines moving and living across the continental springtime from Spain all the way to the season's finale in Moscow (146). Berlin holds together in volatile juxtaposition what Hamburg and Vienna split as largely good and bad objectives of Fleming's travelogue. As we saw, Fleming would rather be driving to Moscow than spending time in any part of Austria except the Tyrol. "With the total absence of an aristocracy or of any other elite (except for the ski champions), the Austrian bureaucrat, who is essentially a small man waiting for his pension, has complete control of the country" (149). Before moving on, note that the ingredients in this negative profile—skiing and pension or retirement—become ambivalent when mixed into the figuration of a father or the mastermind, which, at the limit, borders on Fleming's own authorship.

Before proceeding to Berlin and then to Vienna, the trip through former enemy territory began along the North Sea coast heading toward Hamburg. The chapter on Hamburg and the trip there is framed by women only in bathing caps and trunks mud wrestling in one of Hamburg's red light establishments. Fleming's view of this good clean fun, which is accompanied by contrasts with the guilty management of pleasure back in the UK and climaxes in the claim that Hamburg is "now one of my favorite cities in the world" (125), coats and filters wartime memories that end up compatible with the inner world of Bond—all the way to their evacuation.[10]

On the way to Hamburg, Fleming kept close to the coast in order to see better "the chain of West and East Friesian Islands—sign-posts towards that group of names—Wilhelmshaven, Bremen, Bremerhaven, Cuxhaven, the Kiel Canal—which possess that authentic ring of ill omen for anyone who has served, however briefly, in the Royal Navy" (121). The last time he paid close attention to this group of islands was in 1939 when he was in the Naval Intelligence Division. He proposed a series of plans whereby he "and an equally intrepid wireless operator should be transported to the group by submarine and there dig ourselves in, to report the sailings of U-boats and the movements of the German fleet" (ibid.). The wartime memories that Fleming "had thought banished forever in 1946" (122) are immediately derided as absurd in the idiom of Bond's own superego. "What nonsense they were, those romantic Red Indian day-dreams so many of us indulged in at the beginning of the war—to blow up the Iron Gates on the Danube, to parachute into Berlin and assassinate Hitler, and all the rest!" (ibid.).

The interlude that filled us in on Fleming's double itinerary en route to Hamburg also interrupted our tour of Hamburg's sex industry. Back in the mud wrestling ring, a winner can be declared and a new scene set: "we proceeded to the bucolic pleasures of 'They also sin in the Alps,' described aptly as a 'Sex Nacht Revue'" (ibid.). There is something disposable about "good clean German fun" (123)—as disposable as the wartime memories it accompanies. "People are cheerful. They laugh and applaud and whistle at a kind of erotic dumb crambo which is yet totally unlascivious. Everybody wandering up and down the garish, brightly lit alleys seems engaged in a light-hearted conspiracy to pretend that 'anything goes'" (ibid.). In sum, "in Hamburg normal heterosexual 'vice' is permitted to exist in appropriate 'reservations' and on condition that it remains open and light-hearted" (124).

In contrast to the disposal service of "anything goes," the inheritance of the father complex, passing as a sibling bond, is attended to differently in Berlin. The one continuity shot in the mass of comparison chops showing Berlin decimated in so many ways by the war (or Hitler's rise to power) is the city's ongoing nightlife specialization in transvestism. We encounter here one of the introjects inside the projection of SPECTRE.

> Now, at the Eldorado, for instance, and the Eden . . . some of the "women" are most bizarre. The one I particularly took to, a middle-aged flower-seller such as you might see sitting beside her basket of roses in Piccadilly Circus, is known as the "*Blumenfeldwebel*." "She" had been a corporal in a Panzer division and has an astonishing range of Berlin/Cockney repartee. Some time ago, when a famous English film producer was working in Berlin, she attached herself so closely to him that she was finally given a walk-on part in the film, and all she was interested in now was to try and get over to England to get another job from him. (137)

Fleming's "German" identification enters via the Tyrol in real time; in primal time, the identification begins in the capital of his death wishes, Berlin, the place of the trans-, the ability of at least one *autos*, one of the "selves" (the majority of which crash) to swerve, to survive the impact of the realized wish, and to travel across and inhabit a time of renewed living. The triumphal drive-across-the-plains text between Berlin and Moscow spans and surpasses the German suicide drive that intersects it. "The Germans are the most dangerous motorists in the world," in particular to themselves (146). Fleming gives us the stats of German self-destruction, followed by an Adlerian diagnosis: "Germanic tension and hysteria, plus that basic inferiority complex which makes every German insist that only *he* has the right of way, lie somewhere behind these tragic statistics" (147).

HE'S NO DRAG, HE'S MY BROTHER: SIBLING BONDS

Before there was Bond, Fleming's older brother, Peter Fleming, was the celebrated author specializing in travelogues. With the Bond narratives, Ian Fleming was able to drag his denied travel writing into spy writing, which is propelled by travel to new locations. That *Thrilling Cities* steps out of the drag is what makes this text so full of symptomatic revelations. The Bond film franchise, in particular the Roger Moore versions, presents spying as the upper-class version of classless tourism, whereby even the hick sheriff from Florida is introduced into globalization, the new habitat of American interests. The accommodation of these latter interests in the projection of James Bond—also in the narratives, especially with regard to the CIA agent Felix Leiter—circumscribes the other sibling bond.

In *Casino Royale*, Leiter supplied the cash that allowed Bond to stay in the game and reverse his loss to Le Chiffre. Leiter's "reprieve" led to an inside view of Bond's cybernetic metabolism, which Leiter thus helped service: "he set his mind to sweeping away all traces of the sense of complete defeat which had swamped him a few minutes before" (89). Pre-SPECTRE, Bond shows emotion, typically, only in buddy moments dedicated to Leiter. In *Live and Let Die*, when Leiter is unable to join him on the next leg of the adventure because he just lost a leg to stand on, Bond, his heart full, sends him the message that he misses him (124).

The German word "Leiter" (cognate with "ladder" and "leader" in English) is the benign German synonym of *Führer*. Like a leader, indeed in the film sense too, Leiter opens up the sidelines of the Cold War opposition following his amputations in *Live and Let Die*. While working for the private sector, he assists Bond in *Diamonds Are Forever* and *Goldfinger*, the two works that pit Bond against underworlds pursuing interests independently of the contest between the world powers. In both novels, moreover, Bond goes undercover as a criminal working for the organizations he seeks to research and destroy. The identification of/with these independent underworlds supplies a transitional and liminal place of respite from opposition, one that would be fully realized in *Thunderball* as SPECTRE.

In *Diamonds Are Forever*, the "lump in his throat" (129) Bond feels as he watches friend Leiter limp off to his car is the gag reflex countering the same-sex identification that American gang members invite as "permanent adolescents" (99), whose leaders, turning up the contrast, are "overblown dead-end adults" (126). Leiter first identifies a couple of these teen hit men as a gay couple: "Some of these homos make the worst killers"—in other words, the best (84). In Las Vegas, one of Leiter's associates turns the gaydar on yet another couple of gangsters, this time belonging to the "Detroit Purple Mob," with which they are color coordinated: "Coupla lavender boys. You know, pansies" (107).

That the teen group psychology of the gangs is hospitable to homosexuals is one detail that gets blown up in the 1971 film adaptation. This at once Freudian and fascist insight into group psychology (as the ready position internal to gadget love) expands on contact with new surges of mediatization. The film version introjects Blofeld but projects him as camp. Hard pressed by Bond's vigilant hunt, Blofeld has commenced fabricating his own doubles as lasting lines of defense. In the course of the film, Bond kills two or three members of Blofeld's doubling franchise. When he isn't surrounding himself with doubles, Blofeld even passes in drag through Las Vegas at one point. To attain the safety of total world domination, he has also taken over the diamond smuggling business; he needs the stones to augment a laser ray that, aimed from a satellite at all points on the globe, can extort payment from the United States and the Soviet Union. The first demo-targets Blofeld selects are located on both sides of the Cold War. It is on his behalf that, throughout the film, a couple of homos are liquidating all the links in the smuggling pipe line, which Blofeld has used up as a one-way line of support. He alone will benefit from this one-time-only application of the stolen diamonds. He can be destroyed, however, not alone but only together with his immediate lavender staff and the doubles. Separated out from Blofeld's destiny, the formula for lavender distinction or extinction in the novel (which the film as a whole performs without thematizing it) is to give these couples of homos therapy or give them death. The one female gang member we meet, Tiffany Case, while not yet one of the inverts, becomes the first in the series of Bond girls who, initially allergic to men because of traumatic abuse in adolescence, is successfully treated by Bond in his new role as heterosexual healer.

Bond's inability to take the American gangster seriously previews his later resistance to an acceptance of SPECTRE as a third-party organization in the Cold War world. Indeed we are thrown for a couple of non sequiturs that SPECTRE would reclaim as loop. Compared to "cold, dedicated, chess-playing Russians; brilliant, neurotic Germans; silent, deadly, anonymous men from Central Europe," the crooks assembled in Saratoga Springs "were just teen-age pillow-fantasies" (71). Back in London, the Chief of Staff tried to instill in Bond respect for his new foes. We are advised that American gangsters rank up there among M.'s worries together with SMERSH and "German cipher-breakers" (18-19). Although the American underworld runs largely on gambling proceeds, its investment in diamond smuggling is, just the same, one of the cornerstones of its annual budget: "Six million dollars a year is good money, and you can bet your life it'll be well protected" (19). The figure rolls off with other details not yet assembled as SPECTRE. Another detail gets its marching orders at the opening of the novel. The scene of contraband transfer in the long chain of exchanges comprising contemporary diamond smuggling bears the spectral datemark of the recent past:

> The pilot was half an hour late at the rendezvous and he was bored at the prospect of listening to the other man's inevitable complaint. He despised all Afrikaners. This one in particular. To a Reichsdeutscher and a Luftwaffe pilot who had fought under Galland in defense of the Reich they were a bastard race—sly, stupid and ill-bred. (9-10)

But it is the lair of the dead-end adult leading the pack of perpetual adolescents that contains the kernel of reality in Fleming's claim (against McClory's plagiarism charge) that he had invented SPECTRE. If he did steal it, and if it was McClory who was inspired by the earlier book, then Fleming stole it back. And yet the WWII details or traumata are not carried forward to the spectral site left non-specific. In the vicinity of Las Vegas, then, along the desert mountain range named Spectre, we learn of the restored ghost town Spectreville, once a silver-mining boomtown (for about two years), now gang leader Spang's home on this range, complete with a going loco.

Picking up where the lavender boys were left off, the homo couple takes Bond to meet Spang on board the train. At first sight, Bond immediately identifies the locomotive as "probably the most beautiful toy in the world" (116). In the final reckoning, however, with the clapboard town burning up in the fire he set, Bond transforms the toy train that comes after him into "the coffin of Mister Spang" (125). The next day the newspaper headlines consign Spectreville as a whole to second death: "Ghost Town Goes West" (129). In this punning reversal, the alternate goal of preservation has been preserved just the same.

The homo couple who survive the cremation of the underworld to track Bond and Tiffany on board the *Queen Elizabeth* are the only continuity shot with Spectreville that the narrative carries forward. Right before the assassins make their move, Bond and Tiffany form their couple. Bond suspects that "most marriages don't add two people together" but rather "subtract one from the other" (135). Tiffany counters that this is an apt concern only if you don't care if the sum ends up being "inhuman." That's how she was sheltered in the teen gang. Now she wants to be "complete," which she can't do by herself. By subsuming the chance of subtraction in a completion that only two can carry out, Tiffany defends the couple as a medium of mourning.

Bond's original worry was that having her as a liaison would not only be therapeutic but would also have to be forever. "His would be the role of the healer, the analyst, to whom the patient had transferred all her love and trust" (130). After rescuing Tiffany and finishing off the homo couple, his thoughts return to the "forever" to which his own coupling is now committed.

Forever?

As he walked slowly across the cabin to the bathroom, Bond met the blank eyes of the body on the floor.

And the eyes of the man . . . spoke to him and said: "Mister, nothing is forever. Only death is permanent. Nothing is forever except what you did to me." (153)

And yet, for the span of this judgment, the undead partner (not himself but also the other) was as good as dead, spectral rather than evil. Rather than let his tentative conclusion stand as a corollary to the title's sentence that diamonds, like death, are forever, Bond signs off with a citation of one of his partner's wry lines, which realigns all the boundaries with and within the inner world of the author's relationship to the Bond: "It reads better than it lives" (160).

KLEIN'S CASE OF HANS & THE SCHOOL GROUND OF CHILDHOOD SYMPTOMS

In "A Contribution to the Psychogenesis of Tics," Klein situates the analysis of Felix's or Hans's tic with regard to her early publications on the role of school in the libidinal development of children and teens. Klein analyzes latency and adolescence almost exclusively as site-specific to schooling. The centerpiece of this relay of readings of schooling, "The Role of the School in the Libidinal Development of the Child," also contains case material from her analyses of all three of her children, which she left out of her first book *The Psychoanalysis of Children*. Klein's point of entry is her consensus with precursors Freud, Sadger, and Stekel: "fear of examinations, as in examination dreams," the focus of the precursor research, can be linked to all the inhibitions encountered at school (59).

Going to school, the primary sublimations are pleasure in speech and pleasure in movement. Schooling is all about channeling the flow of libido and handing over the component instincts to "sublimation under the supremacy of the genitals" (73). At school, "the constantly extending ego-activities and interests achieve libidinal cathexis by acquiring a sexual symbolic meaning, so that there are constantly new sublimations at different stages" (ibid.). As formulated in "Early Analysis," it is with repression and the step from identification to symbol formation that libido gets attached to objects and activities of self-preservative instincts not originally possessing "a pleasurable tone" (86). Thus the spread sheet of sublimation folds out. But the analyst must be on the watch for the renewal of inhibition at every juncture.

In "The Technique of Analysis in Puberty," Klein emphasizes that an adolescent boy's interest in sports can serve to master anxiety. It can also overcompensate for the anxiety, which he masks from himself and others (80). The teenager typically "takes as his models heroes, great men, and so on" (82). Because "they are far removed from him," he can "more easily maintain his identification with these objects" (ibid.). All the while repression can lead to "extreme limitation of personality," leaving the teenager "only one single definite interest" (ibid.). It's the equivalent of the "unvarying game played by a small child to the exclusion of all others." The single-minded interest must represent "all his repressed phantasies"; generally it "has the character of an obsessional symptom rather than a sublimation" (ibid.). In order to "get behind the façade of monotonous interest and gradually penetrate into the deepest complexes of his mind," the analyst must fix the focus on "the connections between minute signs of anxiety in him and his general affective state" (ibid.). According to the case study examples she offers at this juncture, what lies behind the one-track concern with one interest only, often a gadget or mode of conveyance, which can also always be seen to include over-concern for damages to it, are "sexual acts which occurred in childhood" (83).

In the case of Ilse, inhibition encompasses her whole personality and emerged with "a very early repression of her powerful instinct for knowledge, which had changed into a defiant rejection of all knowledge" (88). Her compulsive, unimaginative, monotonous drawings, made by compass according to exact measurements, outline an otherwise abandoned urge to find out about the insides of her mother. Klein finds this further symptomatized in her "aversion to the theatre, cinema and any kind of entertainment" (87).

Her presenting condition was "fixation to the mother" supported by two attitudes, "uncritical docility" and "hatred" (ibid.). To complete the essay-writing assignment for school meant to acknowledge her state of "not-knowing"—not knowing about the parental intercourse or what was inside her mother. "As in many other children, having to write an essay signified for her having to make a confession" (89).

In order "to establish the analytic situation quickly," Klein interprets Ilse's constant smoothing out of the folds of her skirt as a masturbatory attempt to repair her genitals. Indeed, Ilse had been sexually involved with her older brother since early childhood: she felt no guilt whatsoever but detested her brother. Klein's assessment of the sexual sibling bond underscores not the taboo bust but rather the absence of pleasure it shares with her abandonment of the desire to know. In "Early Analysis," Klein states that inhibition of talent results from repression overtaking the "libidinal ideas" associated with the activity in question (77). Because Klein obtained "insight into the relation between anxiety and inhibition" (78), she recognized that it is the task of analysis to reinstate the primary pleasure of the activity (rather than, for instance, to try to remove the inhibition).

During analysis Ilse did at last come to feel guilt and anxiety about the sibling sex, which she and her brother were able to discontinue. But the continuity shot in the background was her fixation on her mother. Thus when Ilse's "heterosexual trends had become stronger and her homosexual ones weaker," "her psychological puberty really set in" (91). This trend could be set by analyzing the anxiety aroused in her by menstruation: the interior of her body together with the children in it seemed totally destroyed.

The presenting problem in Felix's case (according to "A Contribution to the Psychogenesis of Tics") was that he was the "neurotic character" identified by Franz Alexander. (The tic would present itself later in the course of the analysis.) Felix's match with the Alexander profile includes his aloofness to parents, brother, and schoolfellows, a mounting rejection of the external world that reflects a "rather asocial attitude" (107). "Though free from actual neurotic symptoms," he's inhibited in his intellectual interests and social relations (106). Pleasure in movement supplies the bottom line for the developments and fixations in the case of Felix. He's only interested in games. While games were "a substitute for masturbation," castration anxiety was displaced onto his schoolwork (108).

As recounted in "Early Analysis," Felix was pushed into sports when his father returned from the war. At the same time, by the resulting displacement, antipathy to schoolwork developed in the boy instead. "Inhibitions of pleasure in motion were very closely connected with those of pleasure in learning" (82). "Games," Klein observes, proved to be "as sublimation more consonant with his ego" (ibid.). In his and her dis-appointment, then, she seeks comfort or revenge when, rather than identify with him, she identifies Hans as his father's son.

In "The Role of the School in the Libidinal Development of the Child," Klein finds a general inhibition of the sense of orientation in Felix's problems with geography (72). Drawing seemed undoable: he didn't know how to sketch a plan, how the foundations of a building were set in the ground. "Drawing was for him the creating of the object represented—the incapacity for drawing was impotence" (ibid.). Klein points out the "significance of a picture as a child or penis": "It can be repeatedly demonstrated in analyses of children that behind drawing, painting, and photography there lies a much deeper unconscious activity: it is the procreation and production in the unconscious of the object represented" (ibid.).

Felix experienced difficulties "standing up when he was called upon in school" (60). When arguing for a gender difference between ways of standing up, he managed to suggest an erect penis in his pantomime of a boy's way of getting up. "The wish to conduct himself towards the teacher as girls do expressed his feminine attitude to the father; the inhibition associated with standing up proved to be determined by the fear of castration" (ibid.). In the same setting, the boy's fantasy of the teacher falling over the desk and hurting himself represented a "sadistic conception of coitus" (ibid.). Another fantasy involving "how he could manage to achieve a better place in class" (61) included step-by-step removal of the students ahead of him in the class (as in killing them). "Then when, by their removal, he had attained the first place and thus reached the master, there would be no one but the master in the class who would have a better place than himself—but with him he could do nothing" (ibid.). In the footnote she drops here, Klein identifies the master as a "homosexual wish-object" but interprets the impossibility of his removal in terms of the underlying disposition that the course of analysis will subsume by the symptomatic wishes it now strengthens: "this homosexual wish was strengthened by the repressed wish to achieve coitus with the mother in spite of the father—in this case, therefore, to attain the first place in the class" (ibid.). Therefore, Klein continues, the guiding wish to speak from the dais, which would put the master (or father) into the passive role of listener, also carries "the wish for the mother" since dais and desk have "a maternal meaning for him." Because learning signifies coitus, Felix dreads the teacher as illicit object. "Thus the conscious wish to satisfy the teacher by his efforts is combated by the unconscious fear of doing it, which leads to an insoluble conflict that determines an essential part of the inhibition" (75).

Felix's inhibition toward all school tasks displays a stop-and-go rhythm in the course of his homework. He leaves the work undone but then does it at the last minute. In Felix's words: "At first one is very frightened, and then one starts and it goes somehow, and afterwards one has a bad sort of feeling" (63). Masturbation proper can commence at this time "as a consequence of the analysis" (64). As he becomes able to masturbate, his lessons also improve. When he at one point succeeds in copying the lesson from a schoolmate, "he had to some extent secured an ally against the father and depreciated the value—therefore also the guilt—of his achievement" (ibid.).

The tic in Klein's 1925 case study, a series of twitches of the face and head movements, was composed in three movements, each marked by another sensation, that of tearing, cracking, and drilling, each corresponding to another role or identification derived from the primal scene. The orchestration of the tic was first set on the scene of music, in which masturbation phantasies were conducted as explicitly homosexual. "Back from a concert Felix complained that the piano obstructed his view of the artist—like the part of the bed that blocked his view of his parents" (110). His desire to know is fixated on the conductor: how can the musicians follow him since they only have their fingers and he has such a large baton? But behind the homosexual content of his masturbation phantasies, it was possible to discern in numerous details (e.g., his interest in the grand piano and in musical scores) Felix's original identification with his father, that is, "the heterosexual phantasy of sexual intercourse with the mother" (ibid.).

According to Klein, the primal scene everyone starts out with is that of the combined parents, whose concert excludes the child and threatens him inside and out. Only if one can separate out the parents merged down to bit parts—Klein's notion of the combined parents comes down, in a nutshell, to the penis inside the breast—will it become possible for the child to enter into a relationship of repair with a whole object. What becomes legible as open wide in the case of Felix are the parts in the amalgamation of the tic and the underlying object relations: the phantasies of destroying the father's penis included the mother's penis, both of which he would drill into with his own penis.

As her son's analyst, Klein saw the alleviation of the tic of homosexuality as an example of successful treatment. For all their differences, Klein and Adler do meet in the happy ending or adjustment that follows the inside view of heterosexual coupling as the model for relationality, which traumatic experiences only dislodge. Julia Kristeva isn't all wrong or entirely on her own, therefore, when she claims that for Klein, too, relational heterosexuality is all there is or can be in a mourning's work. Thus when Felix shifts from passive recipient to active agent of the so-called drilling that his tic represents and represses, his mother analyst sees a wider range of relationality open up.

The mother analyst explicitly prohibited Felix's relationship of mutual masturbation with a boyfriend in order to alleviate concomitant anxiety that was getting in the way of the development of the underlying object relation. Hans was the only one of Klein's three children not to follow the mother's line of work but to become instead, like his father, an engineer. And yet you know the drill: a climbing accident falls or mourns over parental intercourse short of the frame of survival, success, or succession.

While Klein excludes her estranged daughter Melitta in her work with Hans (e.g., neither Felix nor Mrs. A's son has a sister), she makes a separate peace with Hans via her own mother and beloved brother, who also died a young man, and via the unthematized host of her haunt, her older sister Sidonie, her mother's favorite, who died in early childhood. Meltitta was never to be Sidonie's substitute, not for Melanie, not for her mother, who died just as she had established control over the household of Melanie's marriage with young children. Klein dated her first reading of Freud and the start of her analysis with Ferenczi to the death of her mother. Klein theorized full-fledged Oedipal relations already in the first months of life; in her own case, however, "early development" followed the countdown of three losses into young adulthood.

Mother followed Melanie's sister and brother into the crypt and then locked the door from the inside. Klein turned to psychoanalysis to find protection for an endopsychic projection of the crypt, which she re-finds modified, in theory, as the inner world. The inner world of legible spectral interrelationality admitted all loved objects, dead or alive. The impossibility of first and direct contact with losing is the modified impassibility into or out of her crypt, which the inner text reopens as another form of possibility or passibility.

There are several good reasons why Klein would have taken the opportunity of her analysis of a boy evacuated to the countryside during the air war as the occasion to fashion a document of her approach—it was, she felt, the ultimate summation of her innovations in technique. But the patient, Richard, also offered a retake or reversal of the afterimage of Felix/Hans. When posthumously published in 1961, the book-length document counted as her last completed work. In 1945, though, she already presented a preview of the case in "The Oedipus Complex in the Light of Early Anxieties" alongside the case of a girl's Oedipus complex, for which she turned to the material of her work with Rita/Melitta. Why the return engagement with the Rita material already presented in other publications—and on the occasion of Richard's introduction into her work? There are two reasons internal to the 1945 publication that knock about the inner world. (Externally this publication coincides with the complete breach between mother and daughter, following Klein's triumphant overcoming of Melitta's assault upon her reputation and livelihood.)

When Rita started playing with a doll, she was adamant that she was not the doll's mother: "she could not allow herself to be the doll's mother because the doll stood for her baby brother whom she wanted and feared to take away from her mother" (402-03). There is just a bit of additional material, however, published here for the first time (as the note advertises). It is from the early part of her analysis, which commenced when Rita was not quite three.

> She scribbled on a piece of paper and blackened it with great vigour. Then she tore it up and threw the scraps into a glass of water which she put to her mouth as if to drink from it. At that moment she stopped and said under her breath: "Dead woman." This material, with the same words, was repeated on another occasion. (404)

The lifting of Richard's depression appears to roll back the stone from reanimation of the dead. In the course of analysis, the attainment of degrees of ambivalence in the transference allows "the good mother" to "come to life once more, and Richard's depression therefore lifted" (396). For the most part, Klein and Richard work on his anxiety that his hoped-for attainment of potency would conflict with his "greater hope that his mother could be preserved" (381). Earlier, when first introducing his presenting problems now with school, which he can't attend, now with other children, whom he fears, now with his health, which preoccupies him, Klein states that, whenever his "depression lifted," "life" entered him and he was completely "transformed" (371).

Six weeks into the analysis, there's a break and breakthrough. After Richard returns from holiday with his family, he for the first time shows a differentiated and identifiable concern for the consequences of certain ships going bump in the night, which he likes bringing about in session. For Klein, Richard's identification as a creature of the night marks the spot of relief she is in when she can see him come alive.

> The first thing Richard did with his fleet . . . was to make a destroyer, which he named "Vampire," bump into the battleship "Rodney," which always represented his mother. Resistance set in at once and he quickly rearranged the fleet. However, he did reply—though reluctantly—when I asked him who the "Vampire" stood for, and said it was himself. (375)

THE DEPRESSIVE POSITION

In the essay that followed more closely upon Hans's death, "A Contribution to the Psychogenesis of Manic-Depressive States," which appeared in 1935, Klein takes up her first position, the depressive position, though still within a relay of "psychotic positions"—including the paranoid and the manic (279). The concluding sentence even refers to the obsessional position. In a note, Klein argues that she chose "positions" over "phases" in talking about psychotic mechanisms applied and installed in early childhood because psychoanalysis focuses on normal development and the continued existence of early phases would be strictly pathological (275 n. 1). A position marks a spot of tumescence in the inner world over which phantasy watches/washes.

What this essay shares with the 1940 work on mourning is the manic-depressive state. It is in consideration of this state or estate that Klein's theorization of mourning, the inner world, and haunting applies a foundation of legibility via what Klein refers to several times as modification.

Klein floats, always in quotes, the notion of "the loss of the loved object" (265), which refers to an earlier analysis of mourning in the terms of the "loss" the baby repeatedly experiences with regard to the mother's breast, and which reaches a climax during weaning. Klein expressly separates this "loss" as norm from melancholia. "The whole situation and the defense of the baby, who obtains reassurance over and over again in the love of the mother, differ greatly from those in the adult melancholic" (286). Only early failure to secure the internal good object can equate this "loss" with melancholia: "If the infant at this period of life fails to establish its loved object within—if the introjection of the 'good' object miscarries—then the situation of the 'loss of the loved object' arises already in the same sense as it is found in the adult melancholic" (287).

Fundamental to "the loss of the loved object" as norm is the ego becoming "fully identified with its good internalized objects" while at the same time becoming "aware of its own capacity to protect and preserve them against the internalized persecuting objects and the id. This anxiety is psychologically justified" (265). High anxiety towers above the balancing act between identification and projection as well as between good and bad objects. The notion of the depressive position allows for a calibration of the crossfire between identification and projection. For the duration of the essay, "the loss of the loved object" and the depressive position will be maintained as nonsuperimposable, largely to account for mourning, but it seems clear enough that the interpersonal relations of "the loss" will be subsumed by the intrapsychic "position." Admitted here as a present and pressing problem, mourning still needs to be accounted for before the Kleinian court of reality testing that internalization builds and maintains as a modified crypt.

The child "finds himself constantly impelled to repeat the incorporation of a good object—i.e., the repetition of the act is designed to test the reality of his fears and disprove them—partly because he dreads that he has forfeited it by his cannibalism and partly because he fears internalized persecutors against whom he requires a good object to help him. In this stage the ego is more than ever driven both by love and by need to introject the object" (264). But the other stimulus for an increase of introjection is "the phantasy that the loved object may be preserved in safety inside oneself" (ibid.).

An increase of introjection in regular observance of the phantasy of the object's preservation relies on projection to place "the dangers of the inside" in the external world (264). Introjection comes up for greater use by the ego in the course of making reparation to the object. But when the mechanisms of expulsion and projection lose value owing to "the dread lest the *good* object should be expelled along with the *bad*" (265), introjection comes up for yet greater use by the ego in the course of repairing the object. "When a well-marked cleavage between good and bad objects has been attained, the subject attempts to restore the former, making good in the restoration every detail of his sadistic attacks" (ibid.).

Because "uncertainty as to the 'goodness' of a good object" can slip out of the best supported cleavage, the bad conscience exists with its vampiric bites of conscience (*Gewissensbisse*). How else, Klein asks, are we to understand "the slavery to which the ego submits when complying with the extremely cruel demands and admonitions of its loved object which has become installed within the ego" (268)? According to Freud, these are the bites that preserve the primary narcissism of one's own perfection at the negative-theological remove of self-criticism. Klein focuses instead on the allegory of perfection that rises up to counter uncertainties about the good outcome of the incessant sorting out between the bad and the good: "the ego endeavours to keep the good apart from the bad, and the real from the phantastic objects. The result is a conception of extremely bad and *extremely perfect* objects" (ibid.).

Diverse anxieties attend the work of restoration and preservation. "There is the anxiety how to put the bits together in the right way and at the right time; how to pick out the good bits and do away with the bad ones; how to bring the object to life when it has been put together" (269). Klein hitches sublimation to the perfectibility guiding restoration and preservation when she refers to the "sublimation of the bits to which the loved object has been reduced and the effort to put them together" (270). What holds all piecing together in the face of anxieties is the sublimation of the bits unto perfection: "It is a 'perfect' object which is in pieces; thus the effort to undo the state of disintegration to which it has been reduced presupposes the necessity to make it beautiful and 'perfect.' The idea of perfection is, moreover, so compelling because it disproves the idea of disintegration" (ibid.).

While the paranoid uses his toxic interior as a weapon against the objects he lures inside, the depressive uses the introjection-mechanism "for the purpose of incorporating a *good* object" (272). One patient's phantasy of a tapeworm inside him represented—since, as he emphasized, the worm is bisexual—"the two parents in hostile alliance (actually in intercourse) against him" (273). But the worm hole isn't a paranoid survivalist trap. The worm is subsumed instead by the sense of his hypochondria. "It became quite clear that the different organs he was trying to cure were identified with his internalized brothers and sisters, about whom he felt guilty and whom he had to be perpetually keeping alive" (275).

In the 1935 essay, suicide enters in light of preservation and separation of inner objects as another hallmark of manic-depression, which overlaps with but does not cross the boundaries of the depressive position. Suicide can aim "at saving its loved objects, internal or external" (276).

> In other cases, suicide seems to be determined by the same type of phantasies, but here they relate to the external world and real objects, partly as substitutes for the internalized ones. As already stated, the subject hates not only his "bad" objects, but his id as well and that vehemently. In committing suicide, his purpose may be to make a clean breach in his relation to the outside world because he desires to rid some real object—or the "good" object which that whole world represents and which the ego is identified with—of himself, or of that part of his ego which is identified with his bad objects and his id. (ibid.)

In a note that drops here, Klein links this good riddance to the melancholic's withdrawal of relations with the external world, which, we can fill in the blank, supplies the paranoid schizophrenic's experience of the end of the world. The melancholic suicide experiences an uncontrollable dangerous hatred from which his desperate act would preserve his real objects (276-77). Klein shares the suicide's fantasy of his gift of death and brackets out what she should know better from Freud: it is the sense or direction of suicide that one take along (countless) innocent bystanders on one's way out. At the same time, this reading of suicide presupposes a setting of external reality on the inner world. Only in the intrapsychic world writ large (where the self is alone) could this desperate act of evacuation be conceivable.

By way of anxiety and defences against anxiety, the distinction Klein draws between mania and depression follows and allows for her view of suicide as good riddance. She needs the distinction to attend to the increasing volume of anxiety. In one of her case presentations, Klein shows how "through the internalization of his parents all the anxiety-situations . . . mentioned before in regard to the real parents became internalized and thus multiplied, intensified and, partly, altered in character. His mother containing the burning penis and the dying children (the oven with frying pan) is inside him" (282-83).

For Freud, the manic's hunger has a drive-by, drive-through quality—a quality distinguishing this hunger from that of the melancholic, but only as its verso. In contrast, Klein differentiates mania from melancholia by the manic defenses (as in derision of the object or denial of the anxiety attending the intake of the object), which alleviate responsibility for the same hunger. "The ego incorporates the object in a cannibalistic way . . . but denies that it feels any concern for it" (278). After she ventriloquates the ego deriding its objects, she gives comment:

> This disparagement of the object's importance and the contempt for it is, I think, a specific characteristic of mania and enables the ego to effect that partial detachment which we observe side by side with its hunger for objects. Such detachment, which the ego cannot achieve in the depressive position, represents an advance, a fortifying of the ego in relation to its objects. But this advance is counteracted by those earlier mechanisms described which the ego at the same time employs in mania. (278-79)

Mania's losing proposition to internal objects proclaims their separation through mastery: "By mastering his objects the manic person imagines he will prevent them not only from injuring himself but from being a danger to one another. His mastery is to enable him particularly to prevent dangerous coitus between the parents he has internalized and their death within him" (278). To separate this dangerous doubling at the border, the internal objects can be killed and then brought back to life: "One of my patients spoke of this process as 'keeping them in suspended animation'" (ibid.). Klein underscores a certain fantastic mastery of objects under the aegis of omnipotence. But this mastery is staggered by what it promotes: the typically obsessional separation of the internalized parents or the more fully manic alternation between the destruction and reanimation of objects.

Klein's interpretation of suicide is a stopgap that interrupts the abyssal consequences of her reading of good and bad up to this turning point. In this essay, she introduces the depressive position, whereby she will succeed in shoring up the inner world beyond or without recourse to a revalorization of suicide as *Liebestod* or love-death committed to stop "distress about the impending death of the incorporated objects." What heads off Klein's 1935 essay at the impasse of suicide and rescues it as a trial run of the theory of the inner world are the increasing "tendencies to restoration" associated with the newly introduced depressive position. Furthermore, the prospect of impending death, which comes up repeatedly in this transitional essay, is abandoned in the 1940 essay on mourning. In Freud's theory, as in Klein's mourning essay, impending death has no place of its own outside the precincts of the death wish.

TRIAL RUNS OF THE MASTERMIND

That SPECTRE slides into place as an endopsychic projection of the vulnerable but ever reparable repository of losses and traumata—the inner world—can be appreciated anew when we assess the rehearsals of the role of Blofeld. When Blofeld becomes "the Big One" (182) for Bond in *On Her Majesty's Secret Service* after he escapes the destruction of his Swiss operation (but before he appears as half of a couple in the car with Irma Bunt), we catch a glimpse of his figural incorporation of Mr. Big, the mastermind in Fleming's second novel, which bears in its title, *Live and Let Die*, the cybernetic equation of Bond's pre-SPECTRE mode of survival. Like Dr. No, Mr. Big is a third-world/European half-breed; unlike Dr. No, he is in no part German, but half French. He was also born in Haiti and is part voodoo in his psychic makeup. In WWII, Mr. Big was deployed by the American Office of Strategic Services for covert operations in various ports against the collaborationist French. At the onset of the Cold War, he took the Soviet side, placing his voodoo-protected "machine" in the service of assassination and money laundering for SMERSH.

Mr. Big and his machine occupy the cornerstone of another traumatic history to which Bond stands in a skewed line of identification. As he goes through the "purgatory" (7) of customs at New York's Idlewild airport on his first time back to the United States "since the war" (9), Bond takes no comfort in security checks or being on record: "he felt like a Negro whose shadow has been stolen by the witchdoctor" (7). The white world is in agreement that the time is now changing for the black world. In addition to the new black leaders in countless fields, it's time for a world-class black criminal.

With Bond in Harlem, we too are immersed in the already turbulent prehistory of the Black Power movement that the 1973 film adaptation (which restarted the film franchise with the introduction of Roger Moore) uses to update the book. Mr. Big's secret society is protected and projected as voodoo. In Haiti, voodoo operated historically and fundamentally both as a secret society, in which recursive relations to power or energy were promoted, and as a death cult, in which contact with the dead was the necessary part of containing and dislodging traumata that could be sent back or reversed along their primal itinerary (through, under, and across the sea) back to Africa. This aspect is fully intact in Fleming's novel, even more so perhaps, because the voodoo covers for a redistribution of the unearthed loot of English pirates as free money funding the activities of SMERSH. The third-party position of SPECTRE, however, enters the film adaptation through a new plot for the hip-hugging culture of voodoo and jive. Free drugs, rather than free money, are to be distributed, not in support of Soviet espionage efforts but to detonate the Mafia oppositions that dominate the drug trade.

Mr. Big is inspired by a certain impasse, which is historical, moral, but also, inevitably, as we've seen, intrapsychic.

> Mister Bond, I suffer from boredom. I am a prey to what the early Christians called "accidie," the deadly lethargy that envelops those who are sated, those who have no more desires. I am absolutely pre-eminent in my chosen profession, trusted by those who occasionally employ my talents, feared and instantly obeyed by those whom I myself employ. I have, literally, no more worlds to conquer within my chosen orbit. Alas, it is too late in my life to change that orbit for another one, and since power is the goal of all ambition it is unlikely that I could possibly acquire more power in another sphere than I already possess in this one. (51)

In his closing of accounts with Bond, Mr. Big declares himself a superhuman (not by name but by contrast with the "herd") who has "an infinite capacity for taking pains. Not dull, plodding pains, but artistic, subtle pains" (145). By "taking pains," he acquires more power. This is the big part of voodoo he observes. But he instrumentalizes the death cult aspects. He advertises himself as the zombie of the voodoo God of the Cemeteries, Baron Samedi. He thus also advertises a misconception, namely that the already dead cannot be killed.

His in-house medium and betrothed, Solitaire, has telepathic powers that extend into the future. Because the future momentum extends also into the past, Mr. Big ignores this telepathic trajectory and employs her solely to determine whether a questioned person's responses are true or false. Bond, too, ignores her fortunetelling talent. The film version adds the conceit that Solitaire will lose her occult gifts with her virginity, which is why she is kept intact by Mr. Big to augment his control until their retirement from the power machine. The interpersonal relationship between Solitaire and Bond on screen is the uncomplicated sort, which Bond must however maintain under covers because the intimacy complicates his main mission.

Fleming's Bond can miss Leiter because the American took the hit of castration for him, and he can desire Solitaire, who loves him, because consummation has been deferred. In the end, he decides not to wait for all his injuries to heal but to place himself as a baby in her maternal care: "And you'll have to look after me very well because I shan't be able to make love with only one arm" (159). "What about my back?" she counters, and places them both under the nurturing care of the maternal bond (ibid.). In Kleinian terms, with the good sex there will be no love lost.

Bond finds a cave accessible only through the sea which he imagines the pirate Bloody Morgan secured and improved upon for concealment of his treasure. After this recess was fashioned or finished by slaves, the pirate, Bond is certain, would have drowned them all, "gagged for ever with water," "to join the bodies of other witnesses" (137). Pirate industry as a split-off double for the seafaring efforts of the British Empire crowds out the natural "hazards of the sea" with its "great library of books one cannot read" (120).

The Hamletian frontier between first and second deaths opened wide in the withdrawal of Christian controls provided a more flexible or resilient medium of renewed access to the world of our own making than was afforded by Doctor

Faustus's magic. Spirits of the dead are the first representatives of new velocities of production and transmission at "the speed of thought." But in the seventeenth and eighteenth centuries, the enslavement of the dead, who obey the telecommand of one's wishes, does not compare in efficiency (given the outsourcing demands of Empire) to putting slaves to work in the spot of interchangeability that they were in with spooks. Like ghosts, slaves are controlled by the second death that the owner of the magic book or of technological powers wields over them. In *Hamlet*, the stage was set to sail out to colonize a new maritime empire, which will turn the other or new world into narcissistic supplies for the old one, a transfer mediated only by the ghostliness of slave labor. Slave narratives stacking up in the archives of the unread are constitutively ghost narratives. Every slave narrative begins: I am dead.

Like New York customs at the novel's point of entry, the undersea world of passage and recording can switch into something entirely inimical. Fleming folds out of these recesses of reference an Elizabethan spread of vanitas imagery.

> Suddenly he loathed and feared the sea and everything in it. The millions of tiny antennae that would stir and point as he went by that night, the eyes that would wake and watch him, the pulses that would miss for the hundredth of a second and then go beating quietly on, the jelly tendrils that would grope and reach for him, as blind in the light as in the dark. He would be walking through thousands of millions of secrets. (129)

The final pageant shows Mr. Big's machine at work on Bloody Morgan's treasure. Fleming updates it as fitting an arcade: "at once all the figures started moving as if a penny had been put in a slot" (141). In Fleming's day, amusement park rides in new death cults, like the "Disneyland of Death" (*You Only Live Twice* 130), carried forward the close relation between ghosts and pirates. The procession of these pageants begins, however, as Bond's thoughts of mortality bounce up to the destinal stars and down with his plane beset by severe storm winds. He was in flight from the cult of the dying in Florida. American peer pressurization forms society as circles of life self-support. The lowest circle, "the Great American Graveyard," is populated by "oldsters" or "nearly dead" who incite Bond's horror (79). Mr. Big's secret distribution of pirate treasure, hidden in the bottom of tanks of lethal fish, is set within this closing ring of quietude.

If Bond indwells an impasse of identification in *Live and Let Die*, in Fleming's *Goldfinger*, he begins to shake this restraining order by taking it to the secular limits of projection, where SPECTRE, in the subsequent trilogy and, at the same time, in the first Bond films, would get off. "Bond went to his suitcase again and took out a thick book—*The Bible Designed to be Read as Literature*—and opened it and extracted his Walther PPK" (35).

When Bond asks early on about Auric Goldfinger's nationality, we are introduced to a certain double occupancy (given here as denial) attending Goldfinger's every move from background to foreground (both in the book and between media): "You won't believe it, but he's a Britisher. Domiciled in Nassau. You'd think he'd be a Jew from the name, but he doesn't look it. We're restricted at the Floridiana. Wouldn't have got in if he had been" (20). Bond just the same detects the possible admixture of Jewish blood in Goldfinger's makeup (29). In the film version, the hotel where Bond catches Goldfinger cheating isn't restricted and the actor playing the mastermind is German. The golf match is played on screen not for cash but for a single gold bar recovered from the Nazi hoard at the bottom of Lake Topliz.

Just listening to Goldfinger, Bond reflects in the novel, is like "succumbing to ... psychological warfare" (127). Dressed "in the style of German tourists" (141), Goldfinder is attended by an immediate "staff" of ten Germans, three of them "formerly of the Luftwaffe" (251).

The main frame of *Goldfinger* is immersed in filmmaking, by analogy and in fact and function. Earlier Bond narratives use comparisons to movies and to filmmaking, but only in *Goldfinger* does the underworld inhabit the analogical system of cinematic references. Goldfinger flies over the repressed past of what he proclaims for the immediate future as the "greatest crime in history" (186) via film analogies. Goldfinger adopts the cover of film producer for the flight over Fort Knox: "This is Mr. Gold of Paramount Pictures Corporation. We are carrying out an authorized survey of the territory for a forthcoming 'A' picture" (223). In the chapter titled "Journey into Holocaust," Gold receives clearance for his reconnaissance flight, while his accomplice Pussy Galore stands by looking "like some young S.S. guardsman" (224). Goldfinger already arranged to leak into the local water supply a poison first developed by the Wehrmacht in 1943 and then confiscated by the Soviets. He will thus kill "sixty thousand people" (218). In the 1964 film, the reconnaissance flight is replaced with the flying squadron commanded by Galore, which has been ordered to spray over Fort Knox the same incapacitating gas used earlier on the underworld leaders inside Goldfinger's lair.

According to the book, Goldfinger and his assorted underworld allies travel by train to Fort Knox while playing the roles of members of a medical team on a mercy mission to treat the sleeping sickness that has allegedly befallen the population, which Goldfinger presumes dead. Because they are attended by officials and conductors, Goldfinger directs everyone in on the act to look the part at all times. "Apart from the calm, dangerous quality of the man, it was the minuteness of the planning and the confidence he exuded that calmed the battle nerves and created some sort of a team-spirit among the rival mobs" (229). From "the ghostly waiting figures . . . from the gangs" (226) to "Miss Galore with a dozen pale-faced nurses who waited with eyes bent as if they stood beside an open grave" (227), Goldfinger directs a performance that travels the distance it keeps from SPECTRE, coming soon.

THERAPY LICENSE

Bond's license is also a therapeutic one. He treats himself through and to the women he treats. In *On Her Majesty's Secret Service*, Bond's sex therapy with Tracy Lord triggers her mourning sickness, for which he must seek referral out of too close quarters. Bond advises that she be sent "to some clinic, the best there is, in Switzerland probably," to "bury her past" (43). When her father notes that Tracy's Bond adventure seems to have had a therapeutic effect, Bond "gave an involuntary shudder, as if someone had walked over his grave" (40). Does not this grave of one's own refer to a grave that is carried inside?

In identifying Tracy's suicidal depression, Bond shares the sin that fits: she "seemed in the grip of some deep melancholy, some form of spiritual accidie that made life, on her own admission, no longer worth living" (32). Tracy already on her own decided to go to Switzerland for treatment (46). When it turns out that Blofeld, the "ghost" (17) Bond has been tracking, has also gone to Switzerland, we learn in passing that Bond's mother was Swiss (48).

Situated within the "Elizabethan" frame of reference between the two prongs Bond recommends for Tracy's treatment, psychoanalysis and the church (39), accidie also fits Bond as the container to be flushed clean of it. At the start of *From Russia with Love*, for example, Bond has hit bottom: "Just as, in at least one religion, *accidie* is the first of the cardinal sins, so boredom, and particularly the incredible circumstance of waking up bored, was the only vice Bond utterly condemned" (ibid.). That he expels the feeling through a brisk workout separates him from the motivation that the opposition derives from this signal flaw. Without a mission to keep him going, however, Bond, out of boredom at his desk job, even contemplated taking "the unpopular step of entering a minority report" (97). He has of late immersed himself in the administrative paperwork of making controversial proposals. Upon recommendation that a certain number of intellectuals be employed in the Secret Service to catch up with and counter the new trend of "atom age 'intellectual spy'" (96), Bond finds himself defending the prospective appointments against the charge that, since they're pansies, they would be high security risks: "All intellectuals aren't homosexual" (97).

In *From Russia with Love*, Donovan Grant and Rosa Klebb, two out of the three assassin-agents appointed by SMERSH to discredit Bond and unhinge his reputation and mind, are uncanny near-miss doubles or failed introjections of what goes on inside Bond. While a mastermind pursues the intrigue of world domination to stagger and defer his own tendency toward slothful suicidality, the SMERSH assassins work their way out of this decline through murder, which is only a license removed from Bond's own agency, the regulator of Bond's own loathsome inclination to accidie. The product of a fifteen-minute stand in Belfast between a Southern Irish waitress and a touring German professional weight-lifter (14), Donovan Grant discovered in adolescence that he must find a murderous release for "The Feelings" which arise each full moon (15). First he killed pets, then livestock, and finally he engaged the maternal significance of the animal series more directly on a new moon: "he took a chance and cut the throat of a sleeping tramp" (ibid.). That the "tramp" also signifies his mother—the early mother to whom he denies love—is reinforced by the exclusive nature of the release he henceforth obtained. When he comes to kill the occasional girl, he doesn't "'interfere' with her in any way" (16).

He takes the opportunism of his affliction to the Cold War job market. Agreeing "that he was an advanced manic depressive" as well as "a narcissist and asexual" (23), the Soviet clinicians accepted Grant's application for the assassin position. There is always a shortage of executioners; in those not as short-circuited as Grant, the "soul" comes to sicken of killing. "By a process of osmosis with death itself, a germ of death . . . enters the body and eats into him like a canker. Melancholy and drink take him, and a dreadful lassitude which brings a glaze to his eyes and slows up the movements and destroys accuracy" (24).

Upon first contact with Grant (aka Nash), Bond already flexes the greater psychoanalytic frame of evaluation and even historicizes it, another mark of its internalization: "There's madness there all right, thought Bond, startled by the sight of it. Shell shock perhaps, or schizophrenia" (215). What he recognizes in the other as his own is the lassitude or depression from which he tries to distance himself mission by mission. "The voice was even and flat, the sentences trailing away on a dead note. It was as if Nash was bored by the act of speaking" (ibid.).

The in-house evaluation of Rosa Klebb also applies to Grant. Temperamentally phlegmatic, with laziness as her greatest vice, "the Herd instinct would also be dead. . . . She was a lone operator, but never a lonely one, because the warmth of company was unnecessary to her" (62).

> For Rosa Klebb undoubtedly belonged to the rarest of all sexual types. She was a Neuter. . . . She might enjoy the act physically, but the instrument was of no importance. . . . And this psychological and physiological neutrality of hers at once relieved her of so many human emotions and sentiments and desires. Sexual neutrality was the essence of coldness in an individual. (61-62)

If Bond encounters the psycho Grant, SMERSH's Chief Assassin, as a near double, the resonance lurking in the figure of Klebb, SMERSH's Head of Operations, goes deeper inside his intrapsychic body. The communication of this passage relies on Klebb's reputation as a torturer. Through Tatiana's panicked thoughts in anticipation of her interview with the head of SMERSH's Department of Torture and Death, we learn of Klebb's interrogation technique whereby she establishes herself at the breaking point as the mother of pain or its withdrawal.

> She would take the campstool and draw it up close below the face of the man or woman that hung down over the edge of the interrogation table. Then she would squat down on the stool and look into the face and quietly say "No. 1" or "No. 10" or "No. 25" and the inquisitors would know what she meant and they would begin. And she would watch the eyes in the face a few inches away from hers and breathe

in the screams as if they were perfume. And, depending on the eyes, she would quietly change the torture, and say "Now No. 36" or "Now No. 64" and the inquisitors would do something else. As the courage and resistance seeped out of the eyes, and they began to weaken and beseech, she would start cooing softly. "There, there my dove. Talk to me, my pretty one, and it will stop. It hurts. Ah me, it hurts so, my child. And one is so tired of the pain. One would like it to stop, and to be able to lie down in peace, and for it never to begin again. Your mother is here beside you, only waiting to stop the pain." (71)

That this imagined scene based on hearsay is so overlong, detailed, and voiced (the above is only an excerpt) indicates its primal provenance, which won't stay put as Tatiana's history. The draining of courage and resistance that introduces the maternal identification will be featured in the history taken of Bond at the start of *Dr. No*. But the task mistress appears even bigger than the psychic reality of the two of them when she dresses up as the Paris version of Fleming's London mother. "Could this woman possibly belong to SMERSH? She looked so exactly like the sort of respectable rich widow one would expect to find sitting by herself in the Ritz" (243). It is in this guise that Klebb gives Bond the toxic kick (at the end of the novel) that carries the prospect of the superhero's flat line over to the start of *Dr. No*.

At the start of *Dr. No*, Sir James Molony, neurologist to the Secret Service, advises M. that Bond is running out of reserves. Lassitude or sloth may be a cardinal sin, but "courage is a capital sum reduced by expenditure" (17). Beyond or inside the traumatization wielded by his former assignment, the representative of greater psychoanalysis recognizes the pre-Cold War provenance of Bond's depletion. In Molony's estimation, Bond "seems to have been spending pretty hard since before the war. I wouldn't say he's overdrawn—not yet, but there are limits" (18). M. comes up with a vacation assignment as occupational therapy, which, it turns out, harbors the secret plotting of Dr. No. Like everyone else under Dr. No's care or captivity, Bond soon receives the cover identity and designation "patient" (113). The embodiment in one mastermind of the near-missing references to the Nazi era of psychopathic violence scattered throughout *From Russia with Love*, Dr. No was available to the highest bidder, which happened to be the Soviet Union. Like Mr. Big and Goldfinger, Dr. No is interested in what comes before death: he takes great pains with the administration of *poena*, at once payment and penalty. First, he was forced to study his own survival under the castrative conditions of his execution for stealing from the Chinese underworld, which he survived because his heart was in the wrong place. Now, in the meantime, he can apply and extend his findings on torture-test subjects. "I am interested in pain. I am also interested in finding out how much the human body can endure" (150). The arc of his interest in pain surpasses a reversal of the "slings and arrows of the world" (138) he himself endured to embrace the ultimate standard of evil: "I never waste human material. The German experiments on live humans during the war were a great benefit to science" (ibid.).

HAMLET'S GHOSTS:
JACQUES DERRIDA, CARL SCHMITT, ALEXANDER & MARGARETE MITSCHERLICH & FRIEDRICH JÜRGENSON

In *Spectres de Marx*, Jacques Derrida set the stage for summoning and sorting out the different aspects of spectrality within a grid or grimoire of Christian magic:

> To conjure means also to exorcise: to attempt both to destroy and to disavow a malignant, demonized, diabolized force, most often an evil-doing spirit . . . Exorcism conjures away the evil in ways that are also irrational, using magical, mysterious, even mystifying practices. (59)

The scene Derrida opens here belongs properly to the Middle Ages. Rogue clerics, who just wanted to get ahead in a hierarchy otherwise determined by background and training (where they were deficient), turned to a remix of black magic for which they conjured both the Devil's agency of characters and the powers of the good dominating the Christian frame of reference. To conjure demonic forces, it was strategic to keep them in check along the lines of exorcism via the greater force of God. In fact, the magic could be seen to emerge out of this very juxtaposition of evil and good. The envious priests called on God and Satan, much as bloggers throw out "gay marriage" to command the hits list.

But although we would appear to this day to be engaged in magic practices that, from grammar to glamour, rely on curses, spells, and the correct spelling that even the blogosphere's black magic of influence requires for its signature applications, it is a more specifically date-marked haunting that Derrida summons throughout *Spectres de Marx*, one whose provenance begins at the threshold of the secular mind that Shakespeare cathected or occupied with *Hamlet*. Brought before this haunting, we are reminded of the choice that fleetingly crosses Hamlet's mind: is it the identifiable ghost of his father or a demonic impersonation sent straight from hell?

Derrida's study of hauntology held the place of a yet more recent spectral transmission, one that at that time seemed missing in name. But even though SPECTRE apparently disappeared by metonymy with Blofeld, who was rendered forgettable as a punching line of Canadian humor, its underlying significance or impact continues to be stowed away in every attempt to restart the James Bond film franchise. As of completion of this study, the most recent two-part reopening of the projection of the Bond required two funeral plots. From *Casino Royale* (2006) through *Quantum of Solace* (2008), the interpersonal loss of Vesper Lynd had to be worked through to some point beyond revenge. But the inimical force that organizes Bond's reality also functions as the intrapsychic and spectral counterpart to this mourning work. Separated from its measure of grief, Quantum comes to stand alone as another SPECTRE that by any other name still sets a spell with good and evil.[11]

At the first best opportunity, it seems, Fleming sold the film rights to his first novel, which, as a TV movie and then as a spoof, kept *Casino Royale* out of the running of the film franchise that opened up around SPECTRE. In 2006, the franchise sought to begin again by reclaiming, ultimately under the aegis of SPECTRE, Fleming's initial throwaway relationship to the rites of projection in his first Bond narrative.

At the end of Fleming's *Casino Royale*, disappointment in Vesper Lynd's double dealings prompts Bond, now that she's dead, to identify her as disposable. If we witness here the reassertion of the wonderful machine metabolism of Fleming's hero, then a change is wrought after the fact in the midst of the three novels Fleming dedicated and addressed to SPECTRE. At the start of SPECTRE novel number two, *On Her Majesty's Secret Service*, Bond is strapped to a double track. He has been assigned the Oedipal-detective task of identifying what's left of

SPECTRE. Off the 007 track, he ponders early retirement. In this mode of mournfulness, Bond also finds himself tracking Tracy Lord, the haunted mother of a dead child, whom he suicide-watches following their one-night understanding. As the following chapter fills us in, however, the original libidinal upsurge binding Bond to Tracy was set on earlier mourning work. In the second or internalized chapter, we find out about the meantime in which Bond for several years visited the site of the adventure we know as *Casino Royale* and paid his respects at Vesper Lynd's grave. *Quantum of Solace* especially, constructed as a continuation of *Casino Royale* (the movie), signifies the aftermath of Lynd's passing as admitted in passing inside the SPECTRE trilogy.

The sequel borrows its title from a story about the minimum quantum of care, empathy, even identification that is required for two people to be able to start over and repair earlier differences and difficulties. Once bottom is hit, only unambivalent hatred remains (which doesn't make anyone stronger). In a sense, Bond reached this point over Lynd's double betrayal (in life and in death). But the woman in the story who holds this place doesn't die and is instead granted a second chance in remarriage. Toward the end of the movie *Quantum of Solace*, Bond concludes that the dead are not interested in revenge. The woman he has aided in getting even (by killing the man responsible for murdering her family) remains at a loss. But neither on this nor another rebound is she in any way Vesper Lynd's substitute. They part company without even an interlude of consummation. Bond doesn't take revenge against the man responsible for Vesper Lynd's double agency—even though up to this point he has shown himself unable to spare those he should capture for questioning. Another way to put it is that the interpersonal mourning work in which Bond is engaged will come to a successful conclusion— at the very end Bond tells M. that she was right, that Vesper Lynd is his lost love object—and the succession of Bond films can once more fold out of this two-part reopening. But the repository of a solace bigger than the two of them will continue to organize Bond's world in the place that Fleming and the film medium of adaptation and projection reserved long ago as SPECTRE.

It is Klein's notion of the inner world that brings the concealed closure of the crypt into more legible proximity to mourning in a double movement that corresponds to Derrida's reading of the conjury or exorcism basic to "to be or not to be." Klein's systematic account of mourning sought to get around the contradiction in the psychoanalytic treatment of loss. Is "castration" the initiation rite that seals loss in language or substitution as inoculation buffering the psyche in all contact to come with actual loss? Klein's overriding view of psychic reality is instinctual and phantastically represented (at one end) and shared (at the other end) in alternation between external and internal object worlds. This comes to a point in her rereading of reality testing in or as mourning. Since it is not constitutively mediated and muddled by phantasy, the external world is good for allowing the ego to test or prove more readily in the comparison the legibility and reality of the inner world.

SPECTRE's testing of the Anglo-American alliance falls within the transmission of Shakespeare's haunted mourning text unto globalization. Mourning came into translation when *Hamlet* entered German letters, then psychoanalysis, the modern science of letters.[12] It was in this transitional phase that the Elizabethan legacy commenced doubling back until it began to flash forward, together with Faust, as an ongoing beacon of popular culture.

With one exception, Klein approached works of the imagination via translation, including double translation, paraphrase in newspapers. When it comes to the exception, however, Klein promoted translation into English as the genealogical trajectory that illustrated everyman's aspirations to search, destroy, and repair. In "Love, Guilt and Reparation," Klein turns to a sonnet by Keats, "On First Looking into Chapman's Homer," to illustrate processes of early childhood exploration of the mother's body as one's own. Like Chapman his Homer, Keats pronounces his poem's conceit "loud and bold." Not until Chapman's translation could Keats enter the "serene" territory Homer ruled. On reading the translation, Keats feels like an astronomer whose eye is on the sky when "a new planet swims into his ken." But then, back to Earth, Keats becomes like Cortez who discovers, explores, and seizes new land and sea.

> In Keats's perfect poem the world stands for art, and it is clear that to him scientific and artistic enjoyment and exploration are derived from the same source—from the love for the beautiful lands—the "realms of gold." The exploration of the unconscious mind (by the way, an unknown continent discovered by Freud) shows that, as I have pointed out before, the beautiful lands stand for the loved mother, and the longing with which these lands are approached is derived from our longings for her. (335)

Klein can also align Homer with "the admired and powerful father" and identify Keats as his son, who, following the paternal example, "enters the country of his desire (art, beauty, the world—ultimately his mother)" (ibid.). It was to make reparation that Keats subsumed and contained another aspect of the son, the figure Cortez, whose silence, as "with Eagle eyes he stared at the Pacific," signals death (ibid.). The creative work that the artist puts out there in the world is the unconscious restoration of "the early loved people, whom he has in phantasy destroyed" (ibid.).

In Shakespeare's day, English-speaking people set sail on the power of the spirit or ghost become word. Globalization follows in the steps of this projection. In *Moses and Monotheism*, Freud reconstructs the sense of superiority that relies on feeling protected by entirely internalized figures rendered even more fantastic by the stretch of analogy. Freud argues that Moses enhanced and secured Jewish self-esteem not only by the notion that the Jews were chosen but also, and even more so, by introducing the conception of a grander God that invited believers to share in this greatness and feel exalted in turn.

> For an unbeliever this is not entirely self-evident; but we may perhaps make it easier to understand if we point to the sense of superiority felt by a Briton in a foreign country which has been made insecure owing to an insurrection—a feeling that is completely absent in a citizen of any small continental state. For the Briton counts on the fact that his Government will send along a warship if a hair of his head is hurt, and that the rebels understand that very well . . . Thus, pride in the greatness of the British Empire has a root as well in the consciousness of the greater security—the protection—enjoyed by the individual Briton. (*SE* 23: 112)

In Ian Fleming's *On Her Majesty's Secret Service*, M. once again entertains James Bond with stories of his days in the Navy. "Perhaps it was all just the stuff of boys' adventure books, but it was all true and it was about a great navy that was no more and a great breed of officers and seamen that would never be seen again" (146). The end of the British era of the English language's destiny of globalization coincides with the Cold War and the emergence, in the world of Bond, of SPECTRE. Between two sunken eras, that of the German attempt to seize a place in the sun and that of the British Empire on which the sun never set, the Anglo-American alliance divides the work on the past. It is the British secret service to take the brunt of the haunting indwelling SPECTRE for American globalization, which must take and make over the Anglo destiny in all its condemned sites.

Our first SPECTRE sighting on the Elizabethan stage was up against the brink of Britain setting sail into the unknown free-for-all with a swift fleet and kick in the pants of an inertial world. As advertised in Marlowe's *Doctor Faustus*, ghosts are already media traveling or transmitting at the speed of thought. These ghosts attended slave populations and closed ranks with sailors and their pirate doubles. Fleming introduced SPECTRE on the brink of the expansion of Anglo-American mass-media culture going global, often following out the stretch marks of the receding British Empire. To this day, the ghostliness of the Gulf Wars can be identified down to details. But this prospect of nihilism populated by ghosts from secular Hell already scared the id out of Doctor Faustus. *Hamlet* offered a stay against this sheer acceleration of spectrality by installing the medium of mourning at the opening frontier of the other next generation alongside the old magic or new technologies.

For Carl Schmitt, Hamlet, like King James, is lodged between Catholicism and Protestantism and was given to read the ghost in a way that differs from the other two modern mythic figures of bookish derangement, Don Quixote and Faust, who were Catholic and Protestant respectively. Schmitt disagrees with Walter Benjamin on the turf of the notion of sovereignty, which Benjamin borrowed from Schmitt. When Benjamin describes Hamlet's capacity for using Christian images and concepts for illumination of the melancholic condition, Schmitt faults him for driving the hard bargain of dialectical reversal of allegory into intact Christianity that doesn't hold in the case of Elizabethan England. Shakespeare's dramatic oeuvre, and *Hamlet* in particular, is neither of the Church nor political and secular in the sense of the modern sovereign state (62). Schmitt situates Hamletian indecision (ultimately about whether the living Dad is a demon or a ghost) at the border that would prove to be the horizon of the Anglo-American globe. By a momentum unregulated by the theologically neutral sovereign state, insular England followed out its unique historical trajectory into sea power.

According to Schmitt, Hamlet remains the anti-hero of revenge drama because, in carrying forward the traits of Shakespeare's contemporary sponsors, dead and alive, he meets halfway the "taboo" surrounding inquiry into the responsibility of Hamlet's mother, Gertrude, for the murder of the father. While he sees it as an alternative to the psychoanalytic monopoly of the reception of *Hamlet*, Schmitt's taboo reading remains aligned with the psychoanalytic maxim, even according to Schmitt, that every neurotic is either another Oedipus or another Hamlet depending on whether the problematic bond is with the father or with the mother (9). From the quickly dated materials, Shakespeare was able to salvage a kernel of unique historical reality that he raised to the power of myth. The historical-temporal reality was that the new monarch's mother was Mary Queen of Scots, whose intimate intrigues, allegedly extending to rapid remarriage as a widow to the first husband's murderer, wouldn't bear looking into. The taboo brought about the detour that led to the "Hamletization" of the figure of revenge.

Schmitt argues against a naïve historical interpretation of the play. To play *Hamlet* in the masquerade of James's court, for example, would be historical waxworks "or, instead, the attempt to give a ghost blood and a sort of vampirization" (53). Although *Hamlet* is destined as modern myth to exemplify tragedy, the drama's starting position as *Trauerspiel* (and thus as *Spiel* or "play") should not be left behind as superseded. It is *Spiel* that should reverberate in the blank that psychology and philosophy seek to fill. Only as *Spiel* can *Hamlet* bring us before the present of myth.

As Benjamin argued, the first step of allegory is steeped in topicality. Schmitt is interested in the next step, the step that bypasses the allegorization of the present going on recent past. Schmitt attends to the *Spiel* end of *Hamlet*, but he leaves out the *Trauer*, thereby marking the onesidedness of his reception of psychoanalysis. Schmitt feels he has demonstrated the origin of the excess of *Hamlet* interpretations, namely the taboo that creates a gap or impasse into which psychological interpretation was drawn. This draw in turn evidences the mythic quality of the Hamlet figure.

Schmitt's study catches up with Benjamin's inclusion of the Schmittian notions of sovereignty and state of exception in *Origin of the German Mourning Play*. That the study has been measured as a first reception of Benjamin in competition with Theodor Adorno's presentations is also in the service of an elision of psychoanalysis that proves total the more standard it becomes to receive Benjamin's thought as cleansed (through its own prehistory) of psychoanalysis.

Is it *Spiel* or is it Schmitt's own mode of the historical present—of a present that can never present itself in historical dress as continuous or resurrected—that keeps the impasse open? There are two sources of tragic action. The first is myth, which, in the tragedies of ancient Greece, mediates and transmits the tragic action.

The second (and this is how *Hamlet* qualifies as tragedy) is what Schmitt calls the immediately available historically real present embracing poet, actors, and audience (51).

In "Psychopathic Characters on the Stage," Freud also attributes the reception of *Hamlet* to the inherent fit with an audience of neurotics, who are the ones to know one. Since a play is illusion, however, suffering, which alone yields pleasure via any number of transmutations, cannot be inflicted, not outside the compensatory identification with the hero. To this end, a traumatic event must be represented, but buffered as conflict, effort of the will, or resistance. Only psychic suffering underlies the aesthetic or psychological pleasure of the theater audience. Yet as Freud already established in *The Interpretation of Dreams*, the modern tragedy of *Hamlet* contrasts with the Greek tragedy of *Oedipus Rex*, owing to the "secular advance of repression in the emotional life of mankind" (*SE* 4: 264), no longer psychological but explicitly psychopathological. If the staging of largely unconscious conflict is to transfer the psychic suffering, it requires a personalized audience (which, given the secular advance of repression, is available). Neurotics alone can derive pleasure from the revelation of a repressed impulse. When *Hamlet* is performed, the actors will have already taken the audience home with them.

According to Schmitt, the staggered references to King James and his mother, Mary Stuart, play on what every Londoner in the audience thought he knew at that time. But the encrypted theater setting inside each performance of *Hamlet* cannot be brought to light in a matching historical production set on the court of King James. The historically real present cannot be fixed in the historical past. Nor can it be updated. Doesn't Schmitt bring his own internalized consensus and scene to this study, which is the one it takes to recognize the other one? Schmitt plays on what every German in his readership also knows, although in this case, too, the tragic action, the encrypted real historical present, will yield to myth before it allows historical explication. It is a WWII underworld that surrounds the *Hamlet* transmission or machine. To this belongs Schmitt's gesture of reparation to or through Walter Benjamin. As a roundabout possibility, Schmitt follows through the impossibility of mourning in the setting of *Hamlet*'s original performance as in the other setting of Schmitt's own conception and publication of this study.

A decade later, Alexander and Margarete Mitscherlich profited from the impasse that Schmitt's reading of *Hamlet* inhabited by hitching it to the alleged

German "inability to mourn." The missing persons of this work dedicated to successful mourning also returned in 1967. Friedrich Jürgenson's memoirs of his discovery of the "voice phenomenon" restore the complex of unmourning, which Schmitt transmitted intact but undisclosed in his *Hamlet* study, and from which the Mitscherlich couple sought to obtain safe exit.

An artist displaced by the events of WWII from Russia to Sweden, Jürgenson became the talk-show host with the most ghosts via the voice phenomenon: the dead can rearrange white noise, the static between radio stations, even the sounds of regular recordings into communications from the beyond for which the tape recorder serves as the essential answering machine. The recording is in fact all you need to extract the messages from the dead. Just let the tape recorder run, whether in an empty room or outside, then play it back, over and over again; the record that speaks for itself makes contact with the deceased. Jürgenson's first contacts were all with the WWII dead. "Wasn't it remarkable that Hitler and Göring, these two fundamentally different figures, to whom fate granted the leading roles in apocalypse number two, should be making themselves known to me on the tapes? Hitler conducted strange monologues, and Göring sang happily on my tapes" (89-90). What proved especially remarkable was that these dead were all in it together in the recent past: Churchill, Hitler, Göring, his own recently departed loved ones, and Jews otherwise unknown to him. "I followed attentively the tape recording, to the point where the woman's voice with a Jewish accent announced Hitler's presence" (ibid.).

The contact with the departed comes through most selectively when Lena, Jürgenson's radio assistant from the other side, helps tune in the broadcast on the current station. Otherwise contact tends to be with the lowest or outermost region of the underworld, awakening those who died traumatically.

> At first I received a description of the lowest level, the result in fact of a ghastly malformation of the human spirit. One might characterize these aberrations as the direct consequence of a general crudeness in feeling. Its blind power created the grotto-like empty rooms, which my friends designated as *Kavernen* (the Latin word for caves) in the easily shaped material of these spheres. The negatively charged thought- and feeling-waves—above all dread, envy, and hate—shape astral matter, which is readily formed according to wish and the power of the imagination in

exact correspondence to the character of these emotional impulses. . . . Those who were condemned to death by the living as well as banished criminals and scapegoats of all sorts automatically slide into these black cave rooms of the astral level.

My friends reported further that a significant change had been introduced among the denizens of that lower region through the transmission of the radio waves. It turns out that one property of the radio waves is that they somehow revitalize those incarcerated in the dark *Kavernen*. But since the radio waves on account of their mechanical and impersonal nature can bring about animation only at random and in passing, a certain group of helpful spirits (in short, my friends) determined to beam a special carrier wave, across which a better connection to the isolated could be transmitted.

It's easy to get stuck in the "suburbs," as the dead named the outer-lying region of caverns, where the victims and perpetrators, the criminals and the scapegoats are sent first. On the "external" side of Jürgenson's own listening, there's an excavation project in Pompeii. He attends it as a filmmaker documenting the archaeological work for Swedish TV, a double project that stops and starts in alternation with his accidental discovery of the voice phenomenon.

Below me the not yet unearthed section of Pompeii dozes on. Amazing, that it was right here that seven years ago I was to begin the excavation of a house, "Casa Svedese." Instead I penetrated the darkness of an unknown grotto of a spiritual nature. Today, however, now that the "bridge" is already pretty much firmly established, I have returned to the same starting point. (248-49)

The dead deposited in the passageways of the Pompeii-like suburban underworld are the unfortunate ones: without being able to rise on their own to consciousness, they are mired in repetition of trauma. Jürgenson was enjoined by the other side to help awaken these dead and thus break the recycling of pain. That's why contact with the traumatic history of the WWII era rose first to the top of the agenda.

Jürgenson was born in Odessa to parents who were originally from the Baltic States and then moved to Estonia, Palestine, and finally Sweden in the wake of murderous liberations of one ideology by the other one. Jürgenson fully occupies the "I" of the maelstrom of insupportable juxtapositions that he would channel, like Fleming, between haunting and mourning. Many of the friends, dead and alive, who accompanied Jürgenson on his trek through trauma zones of displacement, went down with the Third Reich, but without conviction. The Jewish dead talk to him, too. The ghostly interlocutors speak in tongues, allegedly to signal that it is their contact and not the regular broadcast that is coming through. Usually it's a mix of German and Swedish tossed with some English, Italian, Polish, and Russian words. Yiddish is also one of the tongues, as are Arabic and Modern Hebrew, with which the virtuoso dead reshape the broadcast medium as communications from the other side. What maintains alignment of the voice phenomenon with the archive of haunting is that the covert radio communication can really only get across on record, on tape, which must then be played back and forward until the static clears (often with the help of sound engineers). What was new on the market was magnetic tape, one of the breakthrough inventions of engineering in the Third Reich.

When the German-speaking ghosts fall in line with the recent past, the booming radio voices everyone recognizes of Goebbels, Göring, and Hitler (as well as cross talk from Churchill) are now another kind of live. But there is also a woman's voice speaking German with a Polish-Jewish accent. First Jürgenson can make out a "long drawn out and mocking cry of 'Heil.'" The Jewess remarks with agitation: "That was Hitler—he's not ashamed." It's awkward, then, when she adds: "I mean Hitler—he loves me" (61).

FROM MATERNAL BLOB TO WOUND WOMAN

In "The Psychoanalysis of 007," Fausto Antonini writes of James Bond: "He has no intimate psychological dimensions, has no emotive or rational depth, and everything results in action; he is the hero of behaviourism, always turned towards the external. . . . The past has no hold over him: to remember, to regret, to grow sad, to doubt inwardly, are ailments, when he is affected by them" (105). Bond is therefore "a 'cybernetic' hero" with "the accuracy of an electronic computer" (ibid.). His program: your life is my death, your death my life.

> Here arises the question of the double zero: Bond can kill: but Bond must kill because he can be killed (and his danger of dying, at the unconscious level, is exaggerated by the unconscious hostility of the spectator towards him.) . . . The profound aggressiveness that exists in each of us . . . is entirely directed towards the exterior in the illusion that it is possible to dissolve it by annihilating the 'objective enemy.' The double zero is therefore the illusory and magic but psychodynamically active manner in which, through Bond, the spectator and the reader enjoy their own liberation from the instinct of death. (114)

The range of Fleming's interiors, from the settings of elegance to cells, submarines, aircraft, armored rooms, trains, sewers, pipelines, mines, and so on, shows Antonini that "in Fleming there is, above all, the manifest and typical expression of a repression and of a series of sublimations relative to the sadistic-anal phase of psycho-sexual development" (117). The question of the double zero arises here once more. The public restroom is a place of evacuation, of flushing, to be sure, but also, in theory, it's the same-sex place of sublimational refuge from couplification or even sexualization. In this context, the group bond alone is addressed, the bond that retrieves early relations with the mother. The license to kill, to flush an externalizable threat, also requires or allows for all interiors to be scrubbed clean. Bond therefore relies on M., a mother figure (well before he came to be played or replaced on screen by a woman), who, unlike Christ as Nietzsche stressed out, takes on all responsibility or guilt for Bond's killer assignments.

In Fleming's *Dr. No*, the toxic ambivalence in Julius No's makeup that drives deranged demands for world domination or recognition concerns his German father. While he gives himself the new surname that says "No" to the father, he also incorporates a new first name, a child's name that a mother might call to alert her child to some prohibition, to tell him "no."

Although there is no chink in the armor of a name that denies love to the German father, the name and its appendages must just the same deny the influence of the other castrative threat returning from an amorphous underworld and always trailing behind.

> The thin fine nose ended very close above a wide compressed wound of a mouth which, despite its almost permanent sketch of a smile, showed only cruelty and authority.... The wound in the tall face opened. "Forgive me for not shaking hands with you," the deep voice was flat and even. "I am unable to." Slowly the sleeves parted and opened. "I have no hands." The two pairs of steel pincers came out on their gleaming stalks and were held up for inspection like the hands of a praying mantis.... Bond felt the girl at his side give a start. (130)

What gives the girl a shock fits the film portrayal of Dr. No. But what gives Bond a start, the affective momentum for his showdown with villainy, is the slimy embodiment of evil that precisely does not worm its way into the movies: "The bizarre, gliding figure looked like a giant venomous worm wrapped in grey tin-foil, and Bond would not have been surprised to see the rest of it trailing slimily along the carpet behind" (130).

The guano industry allows Dr. gua-No to convert "bird dung into gold": "And gradually, methodically, my fortress was built while the birds defecated on top of it.... A secure, well-camouflaged base had been achieved. I was ready to proceed to the next step—an extension of my power to the outside world" (139). The anal character, which Dr. No wears openly as his armor's blazon, is also, as a recessive tread of paranoid developments, the defective cornerstone of his securely fortified but externalized place. He never gets out of his military intestinal complex but ends buried alive in the fertilizer.

Dr. No's limit, in other terms, is that he relates to his little critters not as internal bits of the good object, for example, but as subsumed by fertilizer and the swap of excrement for gold. At this station of his development in the novels, Bond spans as a self-cleaning machine a metabolism not unrelated to that of the doctor. But he remains attached throughout his anal ordeal on the fortress island to Honey Chile, who already in name is associated with an early, orally benign rapport with the animal lives of the maternal object. In the foreground of the as yet unreconstructed Bond, however, the ultimate hand-to-hand combat, as devised by Dr. No, pits Bond against a giant squid, the ultimate maternal swamp thing (with "pudding" as one of the giveaway ingredients).

> Bond stared down, half hypnotized, into the wavering pools of eye far below. So this was the giant squid.... Now Bond could see the forest of tentacles that flowered out of the face of the thing. They were weaving in front of the eyes like a bunch of thick snakes.... Behind the head, the great flap of the mantle softly opened and closed, and behind that the jellied sheen of the body disappeared into the depths.... Delicately, like the questing trunk of an elephant, one of the long seizing tentacles broke the surface and palped its way up the wire towards his leg. It reached his foot. Bond felt the hard kiss of the suckers.... Like a huge slimy caterpillar, the tentacle walked slowly on up the leg. It got to the bloody, blistered kneecap and stopped there, interested.... The suckers walked on up the thigh.... Almost without taking aim, Bond's

knife-hand slashed down and across. He felt the blade bite into the puddingy flesh. (166-68)

After he cuts himself free of the castrative suckers and the wounded squid tries to beat him with its retreat by blinding and sliming him with the contents of its black ink sack, Bond undergoes a psychic dissociation whereby he splits or opens up corporeally like an anatomical cross section. We are given ruminations with an inside view of the internal reservations that uncanny or uncontained embodiments of evil cannot but confirm: "The stinking, bleeding, black scarecrow moved its arms and legs quite automatically. The thinking, feeling apparatus of Bond was no longer part of his body. It moved alongside his body, or floated above it, keeping enough contact to pull the strings that made the puppet work" (169).

Bond starts out as another hard body smashing enemies that are represented as slimy decaying bodies or monsters from the deep.[13] He uses his license to kill to run a clean machine: my life is the other's death. Evil is the maternal body or breast grown amorphous and toxic. Then there is a sea change. The specters of this underwater world assume more compact shapes on the screen. In the film *From Russia with Love*, the clearly outlined octopus icon is the secret identification of SPECTRE. Placed beneath a glass of water it alerts the champion of the Oedipal chess match to report immediately to SPECTRE headquarters, which is elegantly mediated by an aquarium's underwater world.

In the 1983 film *Octopussy*, the octopus icon, no longer a sign of SPECTRE membership, marks the warrior maidens of the underworld organization led by the daughter of Major Smythe, who killed himself in the time-out Bond gave him following the discovery of his theft of gold long ago at the end of the Korean War.[14] This film daughter thanks Bond for giving her father an honorable way out. The underworld or underwater organization for women only (based, we are informed, on the ancient octopus cult) turns the goodness of the father's relationship to his daughter, his little Octopussy, as he liked to call her and as she now likes to call herself, into the operation of smuggling the goods past the borders or boundaries of opposition. In the context of the film, this operation is considered sufficiently benign for Octopussy and Bond to view themselves as two of a kind. Unlike the double-0 (i.e., the double barrel clarity that Bond originally carved and shot into the amorphous threat), the octopus icon is singular. Tattooed on one shoulder only, the icon asymmetrizes the Amazon body in association with the legendary removal of the one breast that is in the way of affirmation within the span of her taut bow of the good and strong breast or body.

Pussy Galore in *Goldfinger*, in name and as Amazon pilot, stands out as a model for the film figure Octopussy. In the film adaptation of *Goldfinger*, Bond's seduction of Pussy Galore by appealing to her "maternal instincts" causes Pussy, indeed like a mother, to replace the fatally poisonous gas she was assigned to spread over Fort Knox (the operation is called "Rock-a-Bye Baby") with some innocuous substance. But he also appeals to her as the mother with whom she is instinctually bonded, the pre-Oedipal mother or the good breast. In the book, Pussy, as a proud lesbian, is the ultimate graduate of Bond's practice of heterosexual healing. In several novels, Bond tends to blame the baneful influence of feminism for routing (or rerouting) femininity, which then took up residence in certain men (who tend to be given death).

Tilly, who at the critical moment strays from Bond's protection to seek shelter with Pussy Galore, is also killed. That Tilly's sexual preference already marked her for elimination is given with the image behind the name of the town he fantasized visiting with her while she was still a prospect at his side (140). "Bond smiled sourly to himself as he remembered his fantasies about this girl as they sped along the valley of the Loire. Entre Deux Seins, indeed!" (222). According to Bond, Tilly belongs to the "herd of unhappy sexual misfits—barren and full of frustrations, the women wanting to dominate and the men to be nannied. He was sorry for them, but he had no time for them" (221-22). But Bond has therapy time for Pussy Galore, who as a victim of sexual abuse is treatable, unlike Tilly, whose "hormones had got mixed up" (221). Pussy says that down South you remain a virgin only as long as you can outrun your brother (or, in her case, her uncle at age twelve) (261-62). While Bond now counts as the first man Pussy has met (261), he's going to apply the method of TLC: "It's what they write on most papers when a waif gets brought into a children's clinic" (262).

The Fleming franchise released the movie *Octopussy* the same year that saw McClory release his own film version of the "Thunderball" screenplay. He exerted his rights in contest with the Fleming franchise according to the Court sentencing of SPECTRE's plagiarism or improper burial, but McClory did have to take a new title: *Never Say Never Again*. This 1983 remake of the SPECTRE projection also brought Sean Connery back to the screen during the Roger Moore era of James Bond. In the facing corner of this ring, we find *Octopussy* (starring Roger Moore), among the first Bond films no longer based on Fleming's novels. Instead it took its departure from the story "Octopussy," which was, together with "The Living Daylights," posthumously published in the collection *Octopussy: The Last Great Adventures of James Bond 007*, Fleming's parting epitaph to his specter. In the film *Octopussy*, an Amazon underworld takes over the position of SPECTRE; in *Never Say Never Again*, however, SPECTRE is back and the old Bond is reintroduced into recovery only to be sprung for otherwise inconceivable or unlicensed action as the first Bond to kill a woman.

By restating the formula of his reading, Antonini admits the exception we're pressing towards: "He is directed by others, alienated and alienating, is himself only when he is not himself—that is to say, when his existence coincides with his mission; except with woman" (107). As a killer spy, Bond works behind the scenes to make authority figures look good. But his secret life is directed against the dread maternal body. Then he stumbles on, gets stuck on, makes an exception over the good body or breast. He affirms a throwaway body by wounding or branding it like the animal one spares and keeps close.

In Fleming's story "The Living Daylights," we are granted this exceptional stay of execution. The story is set in postwar Berlin. A Soviet sniper must be stopped from shooting the British agent who aims to cross over to the west. From a room near the border, at once a lookout and shooting post, Bond watches the setting through the otherwise closed curtains while his colleague, Captain Sender, narrates what to look for, what to recognize, what to remember. "It reminded Bond of a spiritualist séance" (72). Waiting around, he loses himself in the tribulations of the heroine of an S/M porno he picked up just the other day in Berlin:

> James Bond's choice of reading matter, prompted by a spectacular jacket of a half-naked girl strapped to a bed, turned out to have been a happy one for the occasion. It was called Verderbt, Verdammt, Verraten. The prefix ver signified that the girl had not only been ruined, damned, and betrayed, but that she had suffered these misfortunes most thoroughly. (79)

Reading matter: reading mater. That's why Captain Sender is the father. "It was with irritation that he heard Captain Sender say that it was five-thirty and time to take up their positions" (ibid.).

Covering the scene with the scope of his gun, Bond catches sight of one member of the orchestra entering the facing building, a woman he sees as good as gone. The "charming" young woman—"vivid with movement and life"—is the unidentified orchestration of vital signs until, upon turning briefly at the entrance, her "profile" is caught in the streetlights. It is a moment of identification, the moment that happens only because it recurs. "And then she was gone, and, it seemed to Bond, that with her disappearance, a stab of grief lanced into his heart. How odd! How very odd! This had not happened to him since he was young" (81). When he was (very) young, he was counted "odd" man out. Your love at first sight belongs to mother. The third person, the father, is the Sender who gets little one ready, set, and going the way of all flesh: substitution.

At the end of the day, Bond's true love turns out to be not only the trigger of eidetic memories but even Trigger, the KGB sniper he was assigned to kill in defense of the life of the agent crossing the Cold War's border. He takes aim, recognizes her, knows that she is as good as dead, but then alters his aim and wounds her hand, possibly removing it. That Bond spared the sniper because she was a woman and, what is more, because she was the woman he had fallen for at first sight, will be on record in Captain Sender's report. Again like a father, Sender apologizes to Bond for doing his duty. His duty is to write down, like the author, this account or story. Bond, however, isn't ready to move on. As their getaway car pulls up, he remains in spectral thrall to the "smashed-up flat," which is reality proof that by contrast the inner world to which Trigger belonged or referred was secure.

> He suddenly didn't want to leave . . . the place from which, for three days, he had had this long-range, one-sided romance with an unknown girl—an unknown enemy agent with much the same job in her outfit as he had in his. . . . She would be in worse trouble than he was! She'd certainly be court-martialed for muffing this job. Probably be kicked out of the KGB. He shrugged. At least they'd stop short of killing her—as he himself had done. James Bond said wearily, "Okay. With any luck it'll cost me my Double-0 number. But tell Head of Station not to worry. That girl won't do any more sniping. Probably lose her left hand. Certainly broke her nerve for that kind of work. Scared the living daylights out of her. In my book, that was enough." (92-93)

He stopped short of killing the woman, wounded her body instead, then embodied the wound and identified with her. The kill or be killed relationship to the externalized swamp—which overflows his inner world and triggers the 00 flushing mechanism—pulls up short before the benign maternal body, the good breast. At the point of identification, this is his embodiment, too. Both the body and the wound are the identifiable objects rising up with SPECTRE out of the earlier primordial wash of threatening maternal blobs targeted for destruction or self-destruction.

Although it takes Fleming several tries before Bond can mourn Vesper Lynd, the throwaway dead bitch from the conclusion of *Casino Royale*, a slip was also already showing in the opening Bond adventure, one that came to be the embodiment of an object relation over the course of the SPECTRE trilogy as in certain stories composed around it. Although it is a more common obstacle in the grammatical course of the English language, Fleming's or Bond's particular lapsus did not go unnoticed. Already Kingsley Amis cited the loose communication of Bond's intentions twice dedicated to Vesper: "As a woman, he wanted to sleep with her, but only when the job had been done" (122). The job would be done inside SPECTRE.

The backdrop for serving Bond straight up with a twist is provided by the masterminds, who are not asexual but bisexual with a dose of fetishism. We know that Bond is fit, with a strong core, through the eyes of Dr. No, who takes a look at his two drugged, undressed guests. After inspecting Honey Chile, he "spent longer beside Bond's bed" and "looked thoughtfully at the hidden strength in the flat stomach" (122-23). What Bond likes to see in his hybrid objects is crossover fitness. Like Honey Chile with her boy butt in *Dr. No* (69), Tatiana in *From Russia with Love* possesses a behind that, "round at the back and flat and hard at the sides, ... jutted like a man's" (68), while, in the same novel, the women combatants in the Gypsy camp display "hard, boyish flanks" (155). In *Diamonds are Forever*, there is one moment of surprise and carelessness that beckons transgression, but that is immediately subsumed by the issue of Bond's professional carelessness, since the man, it turned out, was covertly snapping his picture. Bond tries out the "Oxygen Bar" at the Vegas airport. "He felt nothing but a slight dizziness, but later he recognized that there had been carelessness in the ironic grin he gave to a man with a leather shaving kit under his arm who had been standing watching him. The man smiled briefly back and turned away" (92).

There is a great deal left decontextualized, even smashed to bits, in Fleming's first Bond narrative, which the good versus evil frame holds together in the emergency mode. The development of SPECTRE out of these beginnings must follow the bouncing trans- that Bond/Fleming first slipped into "as a woman" but which the double identity then reclaimed and reconstructed inside and alongside the SPECTRE trilogy. Before there could be a trilogy, *Thunderball* was followed by *The Spy Who Loved Me*, which the SPECTRE trilogy came to enfold.

The search for SPECTRE is on Bond's mind as he passes through the off-season and, in any event, unremarkable (and for him indeed untypical) resort area that is the setting for this love story. The first person goes to the young woman whom Bond rescues while passing through the small world margins of his big world. Vivienne (or Viv) started out in French Canada but, following the deaths of her parents in a plane crash, moved to Europe. In Dear Diary style, her European formation takes the form of her two affairs, one with an English boy, the other with a German man. She is still able to find the history of her affairs reflected back as her newly restored healthy complexion, which had been drained for years in England. In the mirror, she recognizes the successful regimen of "strength-through-joy" (4).

She's just moved in as the caretaker of the resort hotel closed for the season in upstate New York when she discovers that she's the expendable one in an insurance scam implemented by two gangsters. Right before they gangbang her, but after they have already thoroughly roughed her up, Bond knocks at the door.

Later, when they are in it together and the gangsters are busy, Bond tells her about his spy identity, about SPECTRE, and then relates his most recent SPECTRE adventure. His mission was to become, by his remarkable resemblance to the Canadian representative of SPECTRE, a former member of the Gestapo, the enemy's double. "So I took a look at him from a ghost car one day—that's an undercover prowl car—and watched how he walked and what he wore" (124).

When she's intimate with Bond, it seems as if they both like it rough. The only other time we are given the inside view of Bond's brutal eroticism is in *Casino Royale*, though on more symptomatic ground. It's Vesper Lynd's reserve and recess that he wants to break into. In *The Spy Who Loved Me*, S/M is the motto of recreational sexuality, which Viv is quick to adopt as her own: "All women love semi-rape. They love to be taken" (160). It seems rather that Bond was taken. Or did he know he was sleeping with Fleming? To be fair, it would appear that

Bond, too—that is, the Bond who is also Fleming in another drag—also gets to sleep with the Bond. But that is to say that Bond once again makes love in the near-rape style of the mother's strict and absent-minded ministrations to baby, which Freud identified as the primal seduction.

LOVE-DEATH AT THE BORDER TO THE DEATH WISH

Fleming's apprenticeship to his substitute father and to psychoanalysis in Kitzbühel in the Tyrol began upon his return following a second scandalous dismissal from the next school in the UK. He had been there before as his older brother's less serious sidekick. Like a father, Ernan Dennis Forbes offered the mother to treat her son's adjustment difficulties if she sent him to Austria once more. No longer received as the appendage of his dead father's reputation or of his older brother's more recognizable accomplishments, Ian Fleming reportedly came into his own. He composed a first short story during this return engagement titled "Death, on Two Occasions." Toward the end of his career, then, as author of Bond, Fleming went back to where his original impulse to write left off.

"Octopussy," Fleming's last action story, admits living off WWII as a crime awaiting justice, which Bond delivers. The remains of a murder victim have only now emerged out of the thaw of a glacier grave. The dead man, once a citizen of the Third Reich (Austrian annex), had been Bond's pre-war ski instructor and father figure. That is why Bond put in the request to track the fatal bullets to the British officer involved at that time in cleaning up hidden Nazi loot in the Tyrol. Indeed, a certain Major Smythe went into business for himself back then, selected one stash from the documents on his desk, and, after reaching the area, shot his guide in the back to be alone with the Nazi gold.

Fleming shares his Austrian father figure with Bond. He also draws himself as self-portrait in the depiction of the perpetrator of the crime a long time ago. Smythe, who used the Nazi loot to go directly to Jamaica, picking out his wife on the way, is living out his last days in a self-medicated stupor between heart attacks. The cleavage between Fleming's self-portrait as Smythe and the identification with Bond is underscored by the passing reference to Smythe's German mother, who gave him the language skill for the post-war job that granted him access to the Nazi gold over the murdered body of "a bloody Kraut," whose loss didn't "matter" (29).

Wife Mary died two years earlier (in their marital strife she threatened suicide, which she then accidentally or carelessly committed); he misses her love of him. Now he loves the reef fish as "people," which the narrator, being one who knows one, dismisses as symptomatic of loss of contact (13). People who are people in quotation marks, however, aren't really people in the world. Still, the recent turn to the nonhuman (and maternal) sphere of mirroring and "answering" represents the beginning of first contact. Of course, it is too late. Smythe's inner world has taken the plunge, but his "people" are not identifiable or recognizable as his loved ones. His lifeline depends on a splitting image of mother, a small octopus he named Octopussy, a figure primally seductive in part, murderous in the other part. The second, paternal part comes out in Smythe's watch for the results of his experiment with the octopus: "Major Smythe was determined to find . . . [a scorpion fish] and spear it and give it to his octopus to see if it would take it or spurn it." And, if the octopus ate it, would it suffer from the poison? "These were the questions Bengry at the Institute wanted answered, and . . . Major Smythe had decided to find out the answers and leave one tiny memorial to his now futile life in some dusty corner of the Institute's marine biological files" (16).

Major Smythe joins Fleming's identificatory lineup of figures of Sloth, but this time lined up with a death wish that occupies a no-man's land of unidentified dying between the other's death and one's own:

> The truth of the matter was that Dexter Smythe had arrived at the frontier of the death wish. The origins of this state of mind were many and not all that complex. He was irretrievably tied to Jamaica, and tropical sloth

had gradually riddled him so that . . . inside the varnished surface, the termites of sloth, self-indulgence, guilt over an ancient sin, and general disgust with himself had eroded his once hard core into dust. (12)

After Bond has delivered the verdict but postponed the arrest, Smythe proceeds with the experiment. He spears the scorpion fish and finds the fish speared him, too. As the inevitable death by poisoning spreads up his body, he uses his last fifteen minutes to take the second step of the experiment toward the octopus. Yet the tentacles reach not for the fish but for Smythe, whose lips, bitten in pain, left a taste of his blood in the water. Smythe as casualty of this *Liebestod* will be reported found drowned, but everyone concerned will understand as the plain text that he committed suicide. Smythe ends stuck, then, on the combined parents, the double-backed creature inside him. Failing to separate out and establish relations in mourning to each parent and consequently to any complete object, Smythe, on his own or in his couple, recycles "love of him" without identifying or identifying with an underlying object relation. He attempts too late to separate the duo dynamic that embraces him in the love-death of their amalgamation as bit or bite parts. The difference between Smythe and Fleming is that the latter's Bond with father could be rescued from the Sloth or suicidal depression washing up onto the frontier of the death wish. The maternal relation, the other Bond, which follows from the separability of the father and his reinstatement as a loved object in the inner world, informs James Bond's seductiveness as the intent caregiver ministering to baby's basic needs.

With the go-ahead or guidance of Fleming, with Fleming's co-signature, the Bond narrative hits the stage of projection where the haunting on the sidelines now becomes identifiable and recognizable as SPECTRE, the living on of the losses of WWII. The denial attending capitalization of these losses, the whole postwar recovery in a nut-breast, yields to the emergence of SPECTRE. With SPECTRE, Fleming found himself in the close quarters his ghosts gave him; it was high time for making reparations to the denizens of his messy introject.

Appearing first as an underworld of fragmented and amalgamated figures from the recent past ruled by the vengefulness of dead fathers, SPECTRE conformed to the inner world in bits that mourning would eventually restore at its foundations. Thus in the course of Bond's mourning assignment, SPECTRE's underworld organization released the couple (at the busy intersection of missing couples and partners in coupling) as the recognizable format for final reckonings. After the putting to rest of the Blofeld couple, however, *You Only Live Twice* doesn't really end there or anywhere. Bond falls into traumatic amnesia and into the lap of the better half of his undercover identity, his Japanese wife who claims the decontextualized Bond as her own, teaching him to be her baby with a sex manual.

That SPECTRE goes without saying throughout the last Blofeld novel is less a tribute to the one-man show than a measure of the internality of its ghostly organization that is here to stay. Its staying power is the significance of the amnesia that admits both Bond's coupling or substitution and a fully recognizable return to first contact. Freud argued that the heterosexual couple tends to be organized around the man's misrecognition of his object of desire: the Oedipal substitute for mother he is given to recognize in fact attracts him by her pre-Oedipal bond with mother. For Klein, this coupling by misrecognition is what mourning in the couple replaces with the rise you get out of the inner world.

The recycling between the props of funeral and wedding ceremonies was the scandal, the rot, at the start of *Hamlet*, which provided the reading ground for ghostly visitations. As the ultimate test of mourning, Klein reformulated Freud's reflections on the identificatory coordinates of marital difficulties. In Freud's "The Taboo of Virginity," namely the passage from which Stanley Cavell borrowed his affirmative sense of re-marriage for his study of its Hollywood genre, we learn that a husband is still working through his relationship to his father when he's in crisis with his better half, while a wife is still going at it with her mother in her struggles with her man. That's why remarriage, Freud allows, so often succeeds where the first marriage failed. Marriage, for Klein, is always re-marriage, and it succeeds only as mourning, which in this setting means that the internal or ghostly parents achieve integration. In "Mourning and its Relation to Manic-Depressive States," Klein's own proxy, Mrs. A, first felt that "her loss was inflicted on her by revengeful parents." In the course of her mourning work, however, she experiences "in phantasy . . . the sympathy of these parents (dead long since)," who "shared her grief as they would have done had they lived" (359). The tears they share stand for all the bodily fluids to be swapped. Without sexological integration, as Klein argues in "A Contribution to the Psychogenesis of Manic-Depressive States," either parent residing in the inner world can advance to the front of the line of evil spirits as "a dangerous ghost" (283 n. 1). But the ghost must be appeased, not put to rest. Healthy coupling therefore means generous inclusion of the parental pair you bring together again as the individual whole objects separated out in the course of early development from that pathogenic parental combo of the primal scene. For Klein, then, marital sex is shared with these parents, who also get off, internally and eternally, at your pleasure.

DENIAL & VENGEFUL GHOSTS

"Some Reflections on *The Oresteia*" is considered by the editors of Klein's collected work to be incomplete also in the sense that, unlike the two earlier papers on literary and visual art ("Infantile Anxiety Situations Reflected in a Work of Art and in the Creative Impulse" and "On Identification"), it doesn't introduce any new ideas. What's new, and what instills the "confused impression" that the paper leaves on the editors, is that Klein analyzes an identified ghost for the first time. Aeschylus summons to the stage "Clytemnestra's Ghost," who spurs the flagging Erinnyes to keep after Orestes. As Klein underscores, the ghost's appeal to the avenging Erinnyes cites "the contempt to which she is exposed in Hades because her murderer has not been punished" (288). Clytemnestra's Ghost "is obviously moved by continuing hate against Orestes, and it could be concluded that hate continuing beyond the grave underlies the need for revenge after death. It may also be that the feeling attributed to the dead of being despised while their murderer remains unpunished derives from the suspicion that their descendants do not care enough for them" (288).

Klein directly addresses "the belief in ghosts" (288) underlying the relations with the dead in *The Oresteia* in the terms of her theorization of the inner world.

> The Hellenic concept that the dead do not disappear but continue a kind of shadowy existence in Hades and exert an influence on those who are left alive recalls the belief in ghosts who are driven to persecute the living because they can find no peace until they are avenged. We may also link this belief of dead people influencing and controlling live ones, with the concept that they continue as internalized objects who are simultaneously felt to be dead and active within the self in good ways or in bad ways. (ibid.)

Haunting is not a problem of mourning, but one of its tracks, the one that runs deepest. Electra bears libation for her dead father on behalf of Clytemnestra, who places the order following a portentous dream. On the contrary, that the drink for the dead comes from the murderous mother doesn't compromise its purpose. That the libation opens "the parched lips" of the dead reflects the sense that mother's milk is the life not only of the baby but also of baby's internal objects (289). What the external mother bestows on her child is "felt to benefit the internal mother as well. This also applies to other internalized objects" (ibid.). Clytemnestra's children accept that the libation revives the internalized father "in spite of her being a bad mother as well" (ibid.). The bad mother leaves good enough alone. Clytemnestra, who offers the libation through her daughter to appease the father's spirit of revenge, thus revives her internalization in Electra and Orestes as a good object, which in turn brings the internal father to the fore.

> We find in psychoanalysis the feeling that the internal object participates in whatever pleasure the individual experiences. This is also a means of reviving a loved dead object. The phantasy that the dead internalized object, when it is loved, keeps a life of its own—helpful, comforting, guiding—is in keeping with the conviction of Orestes and Electra that they will be helped by the revived dead father. (289)

Otherwise "the unavenged dead stand for internalized dead objects" who "become threatening internalized figures" and "complain about the harm which the subject in his hate had done to them" (ibid.). These loudly communicating ghosts compel both fear and compassion; through them, Klein finds a new opening for the theory of the early superego.

> There is an unconscious awareness in the young baby of the desire to inflict harm on his mother by his greed. As a result the infant feels that the mother has been injured and emptied by his greedy sucking or biting and therefore in his mind he contains the mother or her breast in an injured state. (292-93)

The relation to the mother as an injured and loved object is the source of sympathy with others and the kernel of the hard shell of the early superego. "There is much evidence, gained retrospectively in the psychoanalysis of children and even of adults, that the mother is very early on felt to be an injured object, internalized and external. I would suggest that this complaining injured object is part of the superego" (293). In *The Oresteia*, the Erinnyes lead the procession of injured complainers as manifestations of a superego that runs deeper or earlier than the more recognizable superego figures (under the father's aegis), like Athena.

Cassandra is the liminal figure of the emerging superego shadowed by the death-wish rebound of her prophetic powers. She introduces the problem of denial, the main topic of "Some Reflections on *The Oresteia*." We witness Cassandra in a dream state from which she cannot at first collect herself. "She overcomes that state and says clearly what she has been trying to convey previously in a confused way. We may assume that the unconscious part of the superego has become conscious, which is an essential step before it can be felt as conscience" (294). She is also permanently injured by Apollo's curse that none of her prophecies of warning, which could rescue her loved ones from the disasters she foresees, will ever be heeded. She is lodged by the curse at the border to the death wish. While her prophecies cannot be recognized, she remains a renowned prophetess whose condition of being under Apollo's curse is moreover known.

> The leader of the Elders is touched by her fate and tries to comfort her, at the same time standing in awe of her prophecies . . . The Elders, who are very sympathetic towards Cassandra, partly believe her; yet in spite of realizing the validity of the dangers she prophesizes for Agamemnon, for herself and for the people of Argos, they deny her prophesies. Their refusal to believe what at the same time they know expresses the universal tendency towards denial. (293)

Klein revalorizes denial, the "potent defence against the persecutory anxiety and guilt which result from destructive impulses never being completely controlled," as the underlying disturbance of relations with the injured dead: "Denial . . . may stifle feelings of love and guilt, undermine sympathy and consideration both with the internal and external objects, and disturb the capacity for judgment and the sense of reality" (ibid.).

In "Mourning and Its Relation to Manic-Depressive States," Klein pointed out that "to deny" can mean "to withhold" or "to withdraw." When she refers to "the flight to internal good objects (which may lead to severe psychosis)," she is on the line she had earlier attributed (in "A Contribution to the Psychogenesis of Manic-Depressive States") to her daughter Melitta Schmideberg, who goes unnamed in the mourning essay, though her earlier citation continues to be represented in Klein's discussion of a more widespread than psychotic escape adopted by "people who fail to experience mourning" (368). (On the day of Melanie Klein's funeral, her daughter, a visiting authority on juvenile delinquency, was in London. Rather than attend the service, she instead delivered her scheduled lecture with her red boots on.) The attempt to escape manic depressive illness or paranoia by shutting down one's mourning sensorium leads to a severe restriction of emotional life that must impoverish the whole personality. "Feeling incapable of saving and securely reinstating their loved objects inside themselves, they must turn away from them more than hitherto and therefore deny their love for them" (ibid.). But this denial of "love for them" in the case of the rigid non-mourners also refers to "the love which they deny to their lost objects."

In "Some Reflections on *The Oresteia*," denial is rolled up inside the inverted Oedipus complex.[15] The Erinnyes struggle against Apollo, the sun/son god, the natural born enemy of their mother night. That the destructive impulses toward the mother are displaced onto the father and men in general is the high maintenance cost of the idealization of the mother. "They are particularly concerned with any harm done to a mother, and seem to avenge matricide only" (291). Hence they acquit Clytemnestra of her crime because it didn't involve a blood relation. "I think there is a great deal of denial in this argument. What is denied is that any murder derives ultimately from the destructive feelings against the parents and that no murder is permissible" (292). Every justification of violence, like the sacrifice of Iphigenie as a justification for Agamemnon's murder, is a "powerful denial of guilt and destructive impulses" (294). With regard to the protocols that assigned the Furies prosecution of matricide alone, Klein counters that it is the height of denial to make a value distinction between these dead and those other dead, between these victims and the other ones. It amounts to a denial of love to the good object. Everyone who dies in our midst is the mother.

SECURITY SERVICE

Only in oblivion could Bond inhabit the ego idyll of starting over remarried with a child on the way in *You Only Live Twice*. It is when "Vladivostock" appears in the newsprint recycled as toilet paper that his two-track service (to interpersonal mourning and to the organization of secret or internal security) restarts. Like a client trying to skip contractual obligations to the Devil, Fleming added to this open ending another novel that steps beyond the span of time allotted him and his Bond. The posthumously published and most likely never completed *The Man with the Golden Gun* folds out of the rupture to be continued. In the midst of traumatic memories, Bond returns to the pre-SPECTRE opposition via the portal to the wrong side. First another oblivion must displace the oblivion on Kuro enfolding his marriage to the future, which Soviet intelligence supplies as brainwashing. The KGB realigns Bond like a suicide bomber to remain in thrall to one immediate objective, the assassination of M., which he is not expected to outlive.

M. decides to forgive the ailing Bond—but not to forget. Upon his recovery, Bond must take on another mission impossible to reverse a forgiven but remembered debt. By failing to kill M., Bond also restarts Fleming's patricidal career: he must expiate a criminal intention that was not his own—in other words, Fleming's death wish against his father. M. fits the maternalized image of the father, which, in "A Seventeenth-Century Demonological Neurosis," Freud identified as the deep end of mourning for the father. Bond's target, Scaramanga (aka "the man with the golden gun"), is a hit man for an underworld organization known as the Group, a souvenir of SPECTRE, but with the Soviet Union as one of the major players or members.

We read Scaramanga's profile over M.'s shoulder. It is inspired by Freud and Adler. The traumatic destruction by the police of his totemic animal—the elephant as a figure of never forgetting—set him off on his criminal career. The gun is a fetish that gets its slinger out of the impasse of being either impotent or homosexual. Here we find a collectible but true case of crypto-fetishism that the shellshock epidemic of WWI installed as the reserve of dissociation out of which gadget love and related borderline states could develop and be sustained.

What Scaramanga's fetishism streamlines, according to the profile, is his basic subject position as "a paranoiac in subconscious revolt against the father figure (i.e., the figure of authority)" (37). Among the details of his golden gun fetish, the use of silver bullets occupies an occult trajectory at the border between the human and the animal. He himself is marked by "a third nipple about two inches below his left breast. (N.B. In Voodoo and allied local cults this is considered a sign of invulnerability and great sexual prowess.)" (30). One might add to this profile that Scaramanga's third nipple marks him as a pre-Oedipal composite and combo.[16]

At the end, Scaramanga fills in a blank that makes the scene. A duel has taken place, pitting Bond and his CIA support against Scaramanga's Group, but Scaramanga still survives. He asks Bond to be allowed to say his last prayer.

> James Bond lowered his gun. He would give the man a few minutes. . . . Bond stood there in the sunshine, his gun lowered, watching Scaramanga, but at the same time not watching him, the edge of his focus dulled by the pain and the heat and the hypnotic litany that came from behind the shuttered face and the horror of what Bond was going to have to do—in one minute, perhaps two. (142)

But Scaramanga takes his best shot with a bullet he has doused in poison during the spare time of Bond's stalling. Bond, now in a position as much of mass death as of dueling, twists "like a dying animal on the ground and the iron in his hand cracked viciously again and again" (ibid.). Before he stops to clutch his own pain,

Bond manages to kill Scaramanga. The first policeman on the scene reverses Bond's Hamletian fate: he recognizes the signs of snake poisoning and administers the vaccine.

Bond's impasse shared its fixated focus with Hamlet's inability to move against Claudius in prayer, a scene that is the most symptomatized within the Hamletian frame of references, even those organizing certain case histories.[17] It is the scene of Hamlet's recognition of a certain ethics of haunting: if killed in the Christian position of direct flight to Heaven, Claudius would have been acquitted. Bond/Hamlet can show allegiance only to the figure of the ghost, the contact person of the new secular era yet inhabiting the ruins of Christian belief, but just the same protected against the residual charge of Christian refusal of contact with the recently passed.

That a policeman is in charge of the reversal of suicidality as the precondition for action in the secular world was rehearsed in the vignette of brainwashed Bond's first welcoming reception by the Secret Service. "Such was the ultimate sieve which sorted out the wheat from the chaff from among those members of the public who desired access to the Secret Service. There were other people in the building who dealt with the letters" (14). When we were first introduced to SPECTRE in *Thunderball*, we were also introduced to a certain foregrounding of the function of security. This is what immediately reserved a place for our ambivalence in SPECTRE's receiving area. Behind the address of FIRCO, a French organization founded in commemoration of the Resistance, we witness inimical proceedings reflected in comparisons of Blofeld to Mussolini and Hitler. However, when the deadly discipline of SPECTRE is demonstrated, we are invited to recognize, by way of our own self-discipline, that the question of "security" "affected the cohesion, the inner strength, of the whole team" (51).

We should note the telling denial that follows the inside view of the Secret Service of sorting out between the good and the bad in *The Man with the Golden Gun*: "There was no reason why James Bond, who had always been on the operative side of the business, should know anything about the entrails of the service" (15). But the inner metabolism of his license to kill was what all along was under development: the stricken melancholic world of the clean machine had to give rise, with the rise of SPECTRE, to the profile of mourning. The straight flush of the machine was all along running up against the possibility of loss in games of chance, which placed as the ultimate bet the outside chance or high time of marriage (*Hochzeit*). With SPECTRE, we were introduced to the prospect of living off an opposition that is not one's own. The denied opposition is that of the combined parents whose murderous merger threatens the inner world from within. In relationship to SPECTRE, it proved possible to dispel suicidal sloth by separating and rejoining the guardian figures of the modified crypt. Successful mourning, however, doesn't last long; as an impossible intermission, it must constantly be regained and reclaimed.

Fleming concludes, posthumously, that the work of mourning must fall short of its therapeutic goal of couplification (or integration). At the end of *The Man with the Golden Gun,* Bond seconds the emotion of remarriage. But the suggestion of a Bond of substitution is withdrawn by the concluding "pall" that, by the comparison it shadows, haunts the reflections concluding the book: "At the same time, he knew, deep down, that love from Mary Goodnight, or from any other woman, was not enough for him. It would be like taking 'a room with a view.' For James Bond, the same view would always pall" (183). By the funereal pall of comparison in the close quarters of room for always only one viewing, every substitution is unsuccessful or repeatable. What also remains interminable, therefore, is service to the inner world, which, through Bond's reintroduction via its "sieve," the Secret Service briefly inherits from SPECTRE.

ONLY THE LONELY

In her other posthumously published never-to-be-completed essay, "On the Sense of Loneliness," Klein viewed the titular abjection as the inevitable breakup of the therapeutic aim of integrated development. Among the "roots of loneliness" Klein finds early "paranoid insecurity" and the splitting that defuses it. But the primal defense of splitting in no time leaves both object and ego in bits. Because splitting as egoic defense is only a temporary measure, the ego must come into close contact with the destructive impulses. In other words, the need for integration arises to mitigate hate by love: "The ego would then feel safer not only about its own survival but also about the preservation of its good object" (301).

Klein associates loneliness with the longing for understanding without words, which we feel we came closest to in infancy. We feel that in the beginning we were in close contact, unconscious to unconscious, with mother. The need-to-know basis of being understood by the internalized good object corresponds to another yield: the universal fantasy of having and being a twin. According to Klein, the plight of the only or youngest child is the burden of death wishes directed against the unborn siblings thus barred from conception or birth. In the end, however, everyone is the lonely child who must summon imaginary twinships to bide the long time of the prolonged falling short of integration. Klein presents a patient's field-mouse trip. He caught the mouse as a present for his young child to keep as a pet, carefully packed it in a box inside the boot of his car, and then forgot about it for a day. In the meantime, it had eaten its way out of the box and crawled off to some far corner of the boot to hide and die. The story sparks an association in session with "dead people for whose death he felt to some extent responsible though not for rational reasons" (309). For Klein, the mouse stands for a split-off part of himself as lonely and deprived. By identifying with his child, he also felt deprived of the mouse as a companion. The field-mouse also stands for his good object inside his car, his *autos*, his self. Taking the object in made him feel guilty as well as fearful that it might turn retaliatory. Moreover, the mouse stands for a neglected woman: during the vacation break that had just concluded, not only had he been left alone by the analyst, the analyst, too, had been "neglected and lonely" (ibid.).

The patient was claustrophobic via projective identification into the mother and re-introjection of these tight quarters as a crowding of resentful internal objects hemming one in. Hence he tended to feel lonely in town and free of loneliness in nature. (Although he had indulged in the usual scientific-destructive explorations of nature, like robbing nests, he sensed that, unlike his mother, for whose frailty he felt terribly responsible, nature repaired herself.) He transferred idealization from his mother to nature (308). Throughout childhood, it was his second nature to long for a playmate his own age, a longing that was "the result of feeling that split-off parts of his self could not be regained" (309).

At first, Klein introduces her client (the patient who trips out on the mouse) as the unlikely patient: "a man who was not unhappy or ill, and who was successful in his work and in his relationships" (307). And yet there was this sense of loneliness lingering and malingering from childhood that he still experienced while in town but that he felt he had overcome in relation to the countryside. Through his inner-outer relationship to nature, Klein's "successful" patient comments that he had "taken in an integrated object" (ibid.). But the self-portrait of the successful patient isn't good enough to leave alone. Klein begins again with the internalized dead mouse, then raises the ideal twin, unborn or undead, and finally brings it home, in the transference, as a neglected woman. "The link with similar feelings toward his mother became clear in the material, as did the conclusion that he contained a dead or lonely object, which increased his loneliness. This patient's material supports my contention that there is a link between loneliness and the incapacity sufficiently to integrate the good object as well as parts of the self which are felt to be inaccessible" (309).

Lack of integration must be extremely painful, but the very progress of "integration brings in its train new problems" (301). In seeking integration as a safeguard against destructive impulses, one fears that integration itself re-releases these impulses threatening the good object and the good parts of the self. While undergoing integration in analysis, patients will express the pain in terms of feeling lonely and deserted, of "being completely alone with what to them was a bad part of the self" (302).

Because permanent integration is not possible, one cannot understand or accept one's own emotions. One feels unattractive: one is left alone with unattractive feelings, the bad parts of the self. These split-off parts, often projected into other people, contribute to a sense of not being in full possession of one's self. One doesn't fully belong to oneself or to anybody else. That certain components of the self, remaining unavailable, cannot be regained or reclaimed underlies a pervasive sense of not belonging. To be longing to be oneself with oneself is to enter the alternation between the "ubiquitous yearning for an unattainable perfect internal state" and "internal loneliness" (300).

Though "the facing of internal and external reality tends to diminish it," "the need for idealization is never fully given up" (305). As revalorized by Klein, idealization is no longer the cessation of hostilities that just the same continue; they can be seen instead as fortifying the life-giving primal split between good and bad objects. But this safeguard of the inner world at its foundation is also at risk— and ultimately disposable in the course of integration. The work of integration not only entails losing some of the idealization that had deflected recognition of the destructive, destroyed, hated, and feared parts of the self, which thus endanger the good object, but also lessens omnipotence, which leads to a diminished capacity for hope (304). The realization that no really ideal part of the self exists leads one of Klein's patients to discover and proclaim: "The glamour has gone" (305). What's gone with this specter is "the idealization of the self and of the object" (ibid.).

Idealization defends against excessive envy, the kind that spoils the life-saving cleavage between what's good and what's bad. Setting the bar higher with the ideal, however, you pay this protection by simultaneously risking, through envious spoiling, the inside-out relationship to what's good and strong. Envy of the creativity of mother means destruction of mother's external representatives and ultimately of the very ability to maintain inner and external relations with good objects. The patient is left with "a feeling not only of misery and guilt but also of loneliness in the transference" (306).

Denial of loneliness as defense against loneliness simply shuts down good object relations altogether. The list of factors that mitigate loneliness is long. Klein indulges us only to lower the doom on their outcome. What amounts to one of the best endopsychic descriptions of the near-missing in-group connections constitutive of life in the culture industry, from here to California, is her sense that this glamour that augurs ghostly returns is spread thin for protection against the "longing to be able to overcome all these difficulties in relation to the good object," which is "part of the feeling of loneliness" (305). Klein argues that, whatever fails to neutralize loneliness (generation, generosity, gratitude, enjoyment, independence, resignation, success, capacity to wait, and idealization), gets recycled as defense, even as defensive attitude (309-11). Emptied-out glamour seeks to give shelter to the "extreme cases" of lonely longing, which otherwise express themselves "in the tendency towards suicide" (305).

One longs to be oneself (in California). In the desert surrounding Los Angeles, individuals with aspirations seek out solitude as the elevation of the loneliness in groups on the coast. But that remains a manic defense, which pulls up short before the inner world of mourning and haunting.

Klein's reading of the destinal failure of integration to overcome its defense contact with disintegration brings us before the inevitable "feeling of irretrievable loss" (301). Klein's revalorization of reality testing and integration in or as mourning attended her theorization of the inner world, whereby she sought to contain the recent past as accessible. Following each direct contact with irretrievable loss, the inner world must be reinstalled—this is the essential work of mourning—between inside and outside as a new frontier of the other reality, the reality of loss. From within the empty hub of melancholic glamour, she can also express this loss as mutual, to be sure. Additionally, the plain text of Klein's melancholia, which she sought to entrust to this never-to-be-finished publication, turns around toward an affirmation of a greater relationality basic to the loneliness of endless mourning. In other words, loneliness proves the rule of relationality. "The lost parts too, are felt to be lonely" (302). The constituent parts kept apart by the inevitable shortcoming of integration are parties to a parting that connects them, but as lonely together.

J. K. Huysmans first titled *À Rebours* "Seul" only to drop it for the first of a series of more directional titles that would culminate via Satanism in the protagonist's retirement to a niche of subvention in the Church. In *Là-Bas*, the protagonist's research into the Satanism of Gilles de Rais pulls a limit out from under good versus evil. Evil isn't a plan for perfectibility: it adumbrates the limits of identification beyond which we cannot proceed. Nourished by the evil of the death wish, ghosts nevertheless speak in the voice of the psycho killer who summoned them by magic and murder. Thus too late, Gilles de Rais comes to grief through the evil that kept him in this identifiable world. The recent past, the haunting ground of identification, cannot be left behind except by that perfectible good, which rises up too good for this world, ethically cleansed of this world and unavailable for reunion and recognition. Now that's alone.

CASPAR, HAMLET & HANS

In the year of his mother's passing, Fleming died of his second heart attack (only twice) on the twelfth birthday of his son Caspar, who in earlier years was known to ask his father if he loved James Bond more than him. Bond was Fleming's legacy, but not to his son.

Originally invented for his young son as a bedtime story and then written down while convalescing from his first heart attack, Fleming's children's book *Chitty-Chitty-Bang-Bang* emplaces the gadget love of the Bond world up on the screen within a family's relationship to its magical car. Once rescued from the scrap heap and repaired by the inventor father, the car named Chitty-Chitty-Bang-Bang can fly, float, and save its loved ones. The car is technically the father's prosthesis, but its magical qualities—its uncontrollability and independence—represent as separable the object relation to mother and all others. As a happy medium for the father's relationship to his beloved but neglected son, this story separates out its transmission from its inheritance. In the story's separate Dedication, Fleming pays tribute to an historical car on which he based the fictional magical car. The original car built near Canterbury in 1920 had "a pre-1914 war . . . Mercedes chassis in which was installed a six-cylinder . . . aero engine—the military type used by the Germans in their Zeppelins" (114). Here, in an appendage, Fleming deposits the historical ingredients, German in provenance, of his inner world, but as a foreign embodiment that does not enter Caspar's Chitty-Chitty-Bang-Bang. The inner world, like the crypt it modifies, does transmit, but without interpersonalization: it cannot be handed down. But one man's irretrievable loss is his unlikely heir's ghost of a chance.

When Fleming and 9-year-old Caspar attended the 1961 Disney film *The Absent-Minded Professor*, he left the theater convinced that *Chitty-Chitty-Bang-Bang* had been plagiarized. Thus "The Magical Car" shares with SPECTRE the improperly buried provenance. When Cubby Broccoli (who purchased the rights to all the Fleming fictions except the one Fleming had already sold, *Casino Royale*) got around to making the 1968 musical film version, the story of smugglers interrupted by a family pack on vacation was changed into a Grimm fairy tale of abducted children away at a concentration camp eventually rescued by the magical car and its inventor (the father of formerly neglected, now missing children). In this small European country named Vulgaria, which is made or filmed in Germany using Neuschwanstein castle as its main location, children are outlawed and consequently rounded up by the Childcatcher. The film story is mainly about introducing substitution, a replacement wife, into the schizoid-melancholic father's sensorium and life. In the course of their covert rescue operation, father and second wife-to-be mimic a couple of robot children in love in one of the artificial pageants of childhood performed at court as the acme of the local culture industry. Passing through technologization, not in the absence of life but to rescue the living, the couple becomes possible.[18]

Andrew Lycett reveals that Caspar's mental status after his father's death was suspended between a courtship of attractive and intelligent women and his decision to become an interior decorator. "Stimulated by a visit to Egypt the year after his father's death, he also assembled a respectable collection of Pharaonic antiquities" (449). At school, his main interests were "books and Egyptology." He left university behind to make a career in the antiques business. "Although he was seen with a succession of intelligent girlfriends, . . . his inner life was tormented and he became increasingly reclusive" (451). In 1973, he first laid his hands on the trust money and inherited Goldeneye, his father's estate in Jamaica. In 1974, he went back to Goldeneye for the first time since his father's death. Lycett suggests that he was shocked by the evidence of his father's other life, which his mother sought to keep under wraps. This was one of those times he did not succeed at a suicide attempt.

Before she gave birth to Caspar and married Fleming, the mother had suffered the stillbirth of a baby daughter, Mary. Though fathered by Fleming, Mary was given up to her husband at the time to adopt as his object of grieving. Lycett records Caspar's earlier visit to Goldeneye (at age four): "Ian was concerned that his son had adopted the habit of wearing a hibiscus flower in his ear and calling himself Mary Mary" (308). There was no family model for the name Caspar. According to Lycett, the name was chosen by Fleming as an unwanted name or lost bet. The cartoon figure Caspar Milquetoast, a current reference and butt of jokes for Fleming and his friends, offers a negative, wimpy, and laughable model. That no one would name his son in earshot of this figure was the dare he took. Notwithstanding the difference in spelling, however, it is the American cartoon ghost, Casper the Friendly Ghost, who sets a spell with this name. Created in the early 1940s as the basis for a children's storybook, Casper the Friendly Ghost was sold during WWII to the animation division of Paramount Pictures. The first Noveltoon to feature Casper, "The Friendly Ghost," was released in 1945. Casper wants to make friends with the people he's supposed to spook. He runs away from home (i.e., the local haunted house) to make friends instead. But everyone runs in the opposite direction on contact. The friendly ghost is the lonely ghost. He makes an unsuccessful suicide attempt (he simply forgot that he was already dead); then two children befriend him and take him home. After some resistance, their mother welcomes Casper into the little family. By the episodic status it acquired, the reunion was short-lived, at best iterable. The series, *Casper the Friendly Ghost*, began airing in 1950.

In 1975, Caspar died of a drug overdose, another "mysterious" death that cannot be ruled unambiguously as suicide. The OD victim left behind a note, which is not your usual testament: "if it is not this time it will be the next." While Caspar's parting shot of indifference regarding the first time or contact reverses (and preserves) the typical Bond affirmation of the now as forever (Tomorrow is already dead), the note also shares a curiously upbeat rhythm with the stop-and-go ignition name of Caspar's magical car. The Bond was first introduced between father and son when the latter was conceived as accidentally or unconsciously on purpose: if not next time, then this time. The surprise expectancy of fatherhood led Fleming to enter couplification and commence its exploration as writer of the Bond, initially to assuage anxieties. Beginning with its embodiment of the future, the heterosexual couple was a piece of work of mourning for Fleming. It led to the invention or projection of SPECTRE and, at least within the span of the three SPECTRE narratives, to giving up the vengeful ghost.

Two identifiable losses, the recent deaths of his father and of his son Hamnet, accompanied Shakespeare into the composition of *Hamlet* and the original raising of the SPECTRE between infernal demon and finite ghost. But the leftover Christian frame of reference can be shaken loose and down into the one corner occupied by the ghost in Hamlet's mourning pageant. What is more, ghosts lie. Certainly they participate in the wants and needs of their interlocutors. The murder of the father is less an accomplished criminal act than a painfully current charge of infringement of mourning rites. The second death is that murder of the deceased whose remembrance has been granted only short shrift. An obscenely successful work of mourning attends the *Hamlet* story from start to finish. Claudius's confession of fratricide, like Hamlet's surprise charge against his mother that she first murdered the king before marrying her coconspirator, can be viewed as overdetermined byproducts of the disturbance of mourning. The constant characterization of the remarriage as incestuous also comes out of the disarray of the mourning after.

The ghost in *Hamlet*, as father, commands that the son rerecord or erase the record of his inner-outer archive and sensorium, the volumes of his brain, in order to admit the new medium of mourning. Remember me! No one heeds the ghostly mole. But the moles and blemishes in the maternal face to face, which Hamlet tries to mirror or trap as his sole activity in the service of justice (which doubles back as mourning service only), are bumps in the night or nothingness where all the players are most alive and where they all fall down dead at the end of the Hamlet line of succession. This is not to say that these "moles" are opposed. The maternal shade or echo poses the demand as a question a young child might anxiously ask. Thus the paternal command also transmits a child's quavering wondering out loud if he too will be admitted into this new echo chamber of remembrance and spectrality. Remember *me*?

Where melancholic brooding lets loose, intrigue is required to lace up the mourning pageant in the absence of omniscience or surveillance. Claudius's intrigues are largely linked and limited to the hastened, chastened, and curtailed mourning services he administers to deflect the poison-like contamination of violence from his person and reputation to "the woundless air" (in which it should dissolve). But the heir, Laertes, is wounded more by the shortcomings in the mourning service offered to his dead father Polonius than by the murder itself. Ophelia's enactments of (and in) madness can be construed as her mourning offerings to fill in the blank where her father was to disappear. The king's final intrigue gives Laertes an opportunity to set to sister and father a living monument, Hamlet's murder, under the cover of a secretly poisoned duel. Claudius's motivation or inspiration for the duel, as imparted to Laertes, is owed to a certain Lamord, who praised Laertes's swordsmanship within Hamlet's earshot, which already "envenomed" him with the dual relation. "Let me be your foil," Hamlet tells Laertes. The king's final intrigue, however, overflows its boundaries and objective via the mirroring duel (or duality) of poisoning, the ultimate free gift that comes with group membership, whether in replication or in suicide. At last, Hamlet arrives at the end of a staggered schedule analyzed by Lacan and Jean-François Lyotard in terms of the "hour of the other." This is due in this duel. But the skewering of duality ultimately lies on both sides of the arrival of loss.

Freud set two years as the average span of mourning in "Mourning and Melancholia." In the literature of the occult, both A and B lists, the chronicle of the melancholic or haunted protagonist counts down not in years but in two-year units that mark the failure of mourning (once again) to come to a full stop. It just takes two, even in regard to mourning's curtailment or the simulation of successful mourning. Hamlet lets slip that his mother remarried two hours after his father died. Ophelia corrects him: it was two months. That long, Hamlet exclaims, and still not forgotten!

Hamlet is a play within a play from its outset: the play of Fortinbras, uncle and nephew, overlooks the *Hamlet* mourning pageant on the turf of proper restoration and transmission of the legacy. The beat it thus skips belongs to Hamlet's tale of woe and wounded name recounted or performed by and for those who would conjure or capitalize the new frontier at the border to second death. The functional frame of Fortinbras is its own reward. What gets passed on between the slabs of mourned dead (as filler of sweet consumables at the funeral feast and then, as leftover, at the festival of substitution, successful mourning, second death) is the very allegory of *Hamlet*. The father's ghost was never served. Leave getting even to the Fortinbras frame and name. That leaves Hamlet. He transmits his story for recording and safekeeping to Horatio, whose suicidality must be deferred to this end. When Hamlet junior becomes the ghost—"I am dead, Horatio . . . Horatio, I am dead"—he transmits the tale that lies open before us and around us. Because Hamlet relates to, through, and as the ghost, he stands for work on a new frontier: trial exploration of all that can be undertaken within the relationship to ghosts, the other next generation.

But then there was Caspar, the friendly or lonely ghost who made it inside the very transmission of the inner world without first filling the father's shoes on the outside. He inscribes himself within a mourning process revalorized, for example, as a magical car transmission rather than an inheritance of the Bond. Hans, Caspar, and Hamlet fall through the role of heir to or through mourning while their identification with the specter is as strong in life as in death. Hans, Caspar, and even Hamlet conjure their ghostliness between *The Tragical History of Doctor Faustus* and *Hamlet*, between wide-open reception of media spooks unchecked by mourning and playing posthumous, which reasserts the object relation, but in reverse. Without avenging his father or securing the inheritance of his patrimony, without accepting the identification of the specter as father's single occupancy or bequest, Hamlet transmits the inner world, the identification with ghostliness that transmits him: "I am dead, Horatio . . . Horatio, I am dead." If it is not this time it will be the next.

NOTES

1. When producer of the franchise, Cubby Broccoli, returned to Hollywood after WWII service, he became an agent (the other kind) instead of again taking up his former livelihood as a coffin salesman. The actor destined to carry the Bond forward in the film medium, Sean Connery, polished coffins to make a living before his breakthrough selection as the Scottish representative at the "Mr. Universe" contest of 1952.

2. A certain projective momentum also lies in the background of Fleming's 1958 novel *Dr. No*, which was first written up (in 1956) as a screenplay for a TV show to be titled "Commander Jamaica." When that deal fell through, he concluded the adaptation under the title "The Wound Man." The wound is given with the name No, which the evil mastermind devised and assumed to be a challenge to his German father. It is a patronymic good for nothingness.

3. The first film adaptation of *Casino Royale*, which was made for TV in 1954, cast Peter Lorre in the role of Le Chiffre. One year later, "Peter Lorre" is a comp for the unreconstructed Nazi Krebs in Fleming's *Moonraker*. But the original, we are assured, is more charming. The choice of Lotte Lenya to

play Rosa Klebb in the movie *From Russia with Love* confirms the reservation already made for a spectral ambivalent introject—as forecast on the screen—when Lorre was appointed the first Bond villain. Another premier appointment, that of Ken Adam as set designer for *Dr. No*, also follows the underworld logic of SPECTRE. Adam was 13 when he and his family came to London as German-Jewish refugees. The Adam family owned a very successful high-end fashion store in Berlin and belonged to the inner circle of that city's cultural life. In the undersea elegance of the first SPECTRE operative, we catch a glimpse of the high culture of a lost civilization projected through the apparatus, first of plane flight (he served as a RAF pilot during the war), then of cinema (he commenced film set design in 1948).

4. Fleming also studied Jung's work closely at that time, a reading assignment that completes the reference to what I've termed "greater psychoanalysis," the alternation between reunification and eclecticization of the future of psychoanalysis, first projected as modern psychotherapy at the central institute in Nazi Berlin through the collaboration among three working groups, A, B, and C (the Freudian, the Jungian, and the Adlerian).

5. I leave out Fleming's aside, "whatever else their failings," which denies or proclaims the faults of the Jews. Whatever their faults, "they" won't prevent him from giving them this due. According to Theodor Adorno, however, inside a post-war "German" identification, unambivalent praise for the Jews functions like propaganda, which no one trusts except as the sure sign that something is being concealed.

6. In *Thunderball*, Fleming shares his own birthdate with Blofeld: May 28, 1908 (41).

7. In *Aberrations of Mourning*, I give the close reading of Freud's Julius Caesar Complex.

8. While the shell shock victims of WWI introduced into psychoanalytic theory the upward mobilization of doubling (on contact with traumatization), the victims of Nazi persecution brought home the doubling of trauma to a point

of no return—no return on the investment in loss's deposit, the point beyond or before metaphor and substitution. It is out of the lexicon of Holocaust survival that Abraham and Torok carried forward the concept of the crypt.

9. A striking exception of an overtly repressed continuity shot with WWII can be found in *Moonraker*. This could be one reason it was the last novel to make it into pictures. In the 1979 movie, the Nazi/"not see" element is the eugenics association, which is hard to separate from any listing and selecting of the sole survivors to be admitted onto the flotilla of space shuttles that, like Noah's Arch, carries over the future of the species to the restart position. The movie villain Drax (as unidentified Nazi but open racist) is entirely on his own with his master plan, but the Drax of Fleming's novel pursues his Nazi scheme as outdated revenge, which can be realized in the atomic era only with support from the Soviet Union. The rocket scheme is such a foreign body (as an event in the book and, apparently, as the book) that no one in Britain can recognize a Nazi rocket when they see one being built atop the cliffs of Dover by a team of German engineers. The innocent bystanders can only find it odd that, before one of these engineers shot himself (after assassinating the British detective on site), he shouted out "Heil Hitler!" while giving the salute. The recent past of losses—that past which, but for the repression, would be acknowledgeable as an ongoing tension in the present tense—is covered by a short-term memory loss or dissociation of so tall an order that only group psychosis would fit the bill if, by the logic of the fantasy genre, a shared delusion was not already firing and filling all the blanks. Since the true fantasy at the core of the fantasy genre is that death has died, the match between Bond or Saint George and Drax or the dragon is made in Heaven and does not admit ghosts, nor can it allow what is redeemed as eternal to be linked and limited to the internal world of psychic conflict. Bond misperceives a blinking Shell Oil advertisement as the portent "Hell is Here" (26-27).

10. For reasons not entirely Fleming's own, Hamburg, with its mix of traditional democracy and a sustained aristocracy or elite, is a double of Britain. Fleming is able to comment, with remorse, on Hamburg's catastrophic predicament in the air war since the RAF deemed the site eminently "bombable." "Learning

these grisly facts I remembered how, in those days, studying the blown-up photographs from the Photographic Reconnaissance Unit and reading the estimates of damage, we in the Admiralty used to rub our hands with delight. Ah me!" (126). This concise and contrite history of the air war reaches a happier ending through the interventions of Hamburg's elite, who first undermined Hitler's policy, in the case of their city, to leave the Allies only scorched earth and then interrupted the Allied plan to complete destruction of the harbor in 1946, a plan that threatened to breach the Elbe tunnel. "Long arguments ensued and were only brought to a close by a sporting gesture from the British consul, who took a chair to the center of the Elbe tunnel and sat on it smoking his pipe at the moment when the explosion was due" (ibid.). This rapprochement between Fleming's memories (including "war-time ghosts" [127]) and Hamburg's survival as prosperous and fun-loving, is effective to the extent that it proves hygienically disposable.

11. A good example of SPECTRE's unnamed staying power would be the second film in the reopening season of the Bond with Pierce Brosnan as the leading man: *Tomorrow Never Dies* (1997). But the first film in the 1995 reopening of the franchise, *Goldeneye* (the title borrowed from the name Fleming gave his place in Jamaica), steps out of the Cold War, by then the recent past of new developments in Eastern Europe and Russia, via WWII. This was the continuity shot the franchise had to rediscover after a six-year search. *Goldeneye* is the first film to present a post-Cold War Bond. The double agent in the British Secret Service, who allies himself with another double agent in the Russian military, promotes his own agenda and underworld ultimately as revenge against the British for betraying the Kossacks to Stalin (who executed them for treason) at the end of the war. Brosnan's Bond says it wasn't "our finest hour." Indeed, as a condition for the renewal of vows with the projective medium, the betrayed "our" of various bonding alliances had to come "back from the dead" of WWII.

12. In *Aberrations of Mourning*, I considered *Hamlet* as the translational object in the aspiration of German letters to world literature. That translation thus pressed towards mourning is what I added to Friedrich Kittler's excavation of *Hamlet* between Goethe and Freud.

13. Unlike the proto-fascist Siegfrieds Klaus Theweleit analyzes in *Male Fantasies*, the Allied superhero harbors a traumatic history that is the half-life of any programming imposed or self-imposed to steel the resolve to kill or be killed. Bond comes closest to Theweleit's model in these early portrayals of inimical maternal blobs.

14. Fleming already admitted in *Goldfinger* that the Korean War and postwar Koreans serve as doubles of WWII and postwar Germans on the basis of the division of the land. This becomes an updating substitution within the film franchise beginning in *Octopussy*.

15. The mythic progression of family law in Greek antiquity, which culminates in the transformation of the Erinnyes into the Eumenides, counts three station stops: the dispatched murder of the child, the merger with and murder of the murderous mother, and the inheritance passing from father through daughter to son. In the transformation of matricide into patrimony, it is the prehistory of the missing child that remains the un-understood part and parting. While pursuing the link between the unavenged dead and the internalized dead in the formation of threatening figures in psychic reality, Klein cites one of the harp-player's songs from *Wilhelm Meister's Apprenticeship*. By mis-referring to the citation from Goethe as "Mignon," Klein also summons, closer to *The Oresteia*'s home, another undead child, Iphigenie. In his drama *Iphigenie auf Tauris*, Goethe followed Euripides in substituting Iphigenie's unidentified rescue for her sacrifice, but no one knows it. The paternal inoculation of a shot shock in place of annihilation would build a stronger case for mother murder—did it not rest on the crypt walls of her missing child. Still alive, Iphigenie might as well be her ghost. But then Orestes arrives, following out yet another of Apollo's commands. Between the lines or pronouns, the mission to go to the kingdom that, unknown to him, has served as her sanctuary or limbo and take "his sister" from there to Greece, can be decoded either as the theft of the statue of Diana (his first interpretation) or as the reunion with Iphigenie, which then takes him by surprise. By making contact with his known-to-be-dead sister, Orestes shakes the pursuit of the Furies, whose vengeance is pushed back. They say they avenge the crime of matricide, but it would appear that his own indifference to the loss of his

sister, the loss the mother was presumed to carry inside, was the crime that awoke them. Now that Iphigenie was not sacrificed to the gods, Clytemnestra doesn't have a legacy of justice to (under)stand on. That Iphigenie was living all this time shows that she was both gone and forgotten. Clytemnestra didn't make room for her daughter's absence but used the absence as elbowroom for mounting a maternal and mournful justification for the intimate intrigue against her womanizing husband. The living reunion between siblings undoes the threatening figures, the Furies and the so-called ghost.

16. The 1974 film adaptation is framed by Scaramanga's Fantasy Island, which he shares with the requisite midget; it opens and internalizes the film as a relay of pageants and haunted-house thrill rides that Bond at one point or station identifies as "Grisly Land." Scaramanga, played by Fleming's cousin and Count Dracula icon Christopher Lee, only wishes Bond well: they are two of a kind. Bond was tricked into the initial encounter with Scaramanga by Scaramanga's girlfriend (played by the future Octopussy, Maud Adams), who, creeped or crypt out, sought to be rescued from being fondled with the golden gun. When it turns out, like an afterthought, that Scaramanga has stolen a bona fide gadget for climate-controlling the world, the two of a kind must duel for keeps.

17. Ludwig Binswanger's case study of Ilse comes to mind. I discuss it in *I Think I Am: Philip K. Dick*.

18. Ken Adam designed the magic car for the musical film adaptation.

BIBLIOGRAPHY

Abraham, Karl. "A Short History of the Development of the Libido, Viewed in the Light of Mental Disorders." *Selected Papers*. Vol. 2. 1924. Trans. Douglas Bryan and Alix Strachey. New York: Basic Books, 1960. 418-501.

Abraham, Nicolas and Maria Torok. "Introjection-Incorporation: Mourning or Melancholia." *Psychoanalysis in France*. 1972. Ed. Serge Lebovici and Daniel Widlöcher. New York: International Universities Press, 1980. 3-16.

Adorno, Theodor W. "Was bedeutet: Aufarbeitung der Vergangenheit." *Gesammelte Schriften*. 1959. Ed. Rolf Tiedemann. Vol. 10.2. Frankfurt a/M: Suhrkamp, 2003. 555-72.

Amis, Kingsley. *The James Bond Dossier*. New York: The New American Library, 1965.

Antonini, Fausto. "The Psychoanalysis of 007." *The Bond Affair*. 1965. Ed. Oreste Del Buono and Umberto Eco. Trans. R. A. Downie. London: Macdonald, 1966. 103-21.

Benjamin, Walter. *Ursprung des deutschen Trauerspiels: Gesammelte Schriften*. 1925. Ed. Rolf Tiedemann and Hermann Schweppenhäuser. I/1. Frankfurt a/M: Suhrkamp, 1980.

Brosnan, James. *James Bond in the Cinema*. London: The Tantiry Press, 1972.

Bryce, Ivar. *You Only Live Once: Memories of Ian Fleming*. 1975. Frederick: University Publications of America, 1984.

Cavell, Stanley. "Hamlet's Burden of Proof." *Disowning Knowledge in Seven Plays of Shakespeare*. 1987. Cambridge: Cambridge University Press, 2003. 179-91.

———. *Pursuits of Happiness: The Hollywood Comedy of Remarriage*. Cambridge: Harvard University Press, 1981.

Derrida, Jacques. *Specters of Marx: The State of the Debt, the Work of Mourning and the New International*. 1993. Trans. Peggy Kamuf. New York and London: Routledge, 2006.

Fleming, Ian. *Casino Royale*. 1953. London: Penguin Books, 2009.

———. *Chitty-Chitty-Bang-Bang: The Magical Car*. New York: Random House, 1964.

———. *Diamonds are Forever*. 1956. New York: Signet Books, 1964.

———. *Dr. No*. New York: Signet Books, 1958.

———. *For Your Eyes Only*. 1960. New York: Signet Books, 1963.

———. *From Russia with Love*. 1957. New York: Berkley Books, 1985.

———. *Goldfinger*. 1959. New York: Berkley Books, 1982.

———. "Introduction." *The Seven Deadly Sins*. 1962. Ed. Ian Fleming. New York: William Morrow, 1992.

———. *Live and Let Die*. New York: Signet Books, 1954.

———. *Moonraker*. 1955. New York: Signet Books, 1960.

———. *Octopussy: The Last Adventures of James Bond 007*. New York: Signet Books, New American Library, 1967.

———. *On Her Majesty's Secret Service*. 1963. New York: Signet Books, 1964.

———. *The Man with the Golden Gun*. 1965. New York: Signet Books, 1966.

———. *The Spy Who Loved Me*. 1962. New York: Berkley Books, 1983.

———. *Thrilling Cities*. New York: Signet Books, 1965.

———. *Thunderball*. 1961. New York: Viking Press, 1985.

———. *You Only Live Twice*. 1964. New York: Signet Books, 1965.

Freud, Sigmund. *The Standard Edition of the Complete Psychological Works*. Trans. and ed. James Strachey. 24 vols. London: The Hogarth Press, 1958.

Goethe, Johann Wolfgang. *Iphigenie auf Tauris: Goethes Werke*. Ed. Paul Stapf. Vol. 2. Berlin: Deutsche Buch-Gemeinschaft, 1963.

Jürgenson, Friedrich. *Sprechfunk mit Verstorbenen: Eine dem Atomzeitalter gemäße Form der praktischen technishcen-physikalischen Kotaktherstellung mit dem Jenseits*. Freiburg: Verlag Hermann Bauer, 1967.

Klein, Melanie. "A Contribution to the Psychogenesis of Manic-Depressive States." 1935. *Love, Guilt and Reparation and Other Works 1921-1945*. New York: The Free Press, 1984. 262-89.

———. "A Contribution to the Psychogenesis of Tics." 1925. *Love, Guilt and Reparation and Other Works 1921-1945*. New York: The Free Press, 1984. 106-27.

———. "Early Analysis." 1923. *Love, Guilt and Reparation and Other Works 1921-1945*. New York: The Free Press, 1984. 77-105.

———. "Inhibitions and Difficulties at Puberty." 1922. *Love, Guilt and Reparation and Other Works 1921-1945*. New York: The Free Press, 1984. 54-58.

———. "Love, Guilt and Reparation." 1937. *Love, Guilt and Reparation and Other Works 1921-1945*. New York: The Free Press, 1984. 306-43.

———. "Mourning and Its Relation to Manic-Depressive States." 1940. *Love, Guilt and Reparation and Other Works 1921-1945*. New York: The Free Press, 1984. 344-69.

———. "On the Sense of Loneliness." 1963. *Envy and Gratitude and Other Works 1946-1963*. New York: The Free Press, 1984. 300-13.

———. "Some Reflections on *The Oresteia*." 1963. *Envy and Gratitude and Other Works 1946-1963*. New York: The Free Press, 1984. 275-99.

———. "The Oedipus Complex in the Light of Early Anxieties." 1945. *Love, Guilt and Reparation and Other Works 1921-1945*. New York: The Free Press, 1984. 370-419.

———. "The Role of the School in the Libidinal Development of the Child." 1923. *Love, Guilt and Reparation and Other Works 1921-1945*. New York: The Free Press, 1984. 59-76.

———. "The Technique of Analysis in Puberty." 1932. *The Psychoanalysis of Children*. Trans. Alix Strachey and H. A. Thorner. New York: The Free Press, 1984. 80-94.

Kristeva, Julia. *Melanie Klein*. 2000. Trans. Ross Guberman. New York: Columbia University Press, 2004.

Lacan, Jacques. "Desire and the Interpretation of Desire in *Hamlet*." *Literature and Psychoanalysis: The Question of Reading: Otherwise*. Ed. Shoshana Felman. Baltimore: Johns Hopkins University Press, 1982. 11-52.

Lycett, Andrew. *Ian Fleming: The Man Behind James Bond*. Atlanta: Turner Publishing, 1996.

Lyotard, Jean Francois. "Jewish Oedipus." 1970. Trans. Susan Hanson. *Genre* 10.3 (Fall 1977): 395-411.

Mitscherlich, Alexander and Margarete Mitscherlich. *Die Unfähigkeit zu trauern. Grundlagen kollektiven Verhaltens*. 1967. Munich: R. Piper & Co., 1980.

Ronell, Avital. *The Test Drive*. Urbana: University of Illinois Press, 2005.

Schmitt, Carl. *Hamlet oder Hekuba: Der Einbruch der Zeit in das Spiel*. 1956. Stuttgart: Klett-Cotta, 1999.

Smoltczyk, Alexander. *James Bond Berlin Hollywood: Die Welten des Ken Adam*. Berlin: Nicolaische Verlagsbuchhandlung, 2002.

Theweleit, Klaus. *Male Fantasies*. Trans. Erica Carter, Stephen Conway, and Chris Turner. 2 vols. Minneapolis: University of Minnesota Press, 1987 and 1989.

SPECTRE

"The Big One (SPECTRE)"
Photograph by Nancy Barton (2011/2013)

LAURENCE A. RICKELS moved to the Coast in 1981 upon completing his graduate training in German philology at Princeton University. While in California he earned a psychotherapy license. He has published numerous studies of the phenomenon he calls "unmourning," a term that became the title of his trilogy: *Aberrations of Mourning*, *The Case of California*, and *Nazi Psychoanalysis*. He has also written two "course books," *The Vampire Lectures* and *The Devil Notebooks*. 2010 saw the publication of *I Think I Am: Philip K. Dick*, a schizoanalysis of the science fiction author's life and work. Rickels is Emeritus Professor of German and Comparative Literature at the University of California-Santa Barbara. Currently he is Professor of Art and Theory at the Academy of Fine Arts-Karlsruhe and Sigmund Freud Professor of Media and Philosophy at the European Graduate School.